GW01019417

# *Bobby*

## A YOUNG MAN CLAIMED BY GOD

### JEAN MCDOWELL

**Outskirts Press, Inc.**
**Denver, Colorado**

This is a work of fiction. The events and characters described herein are imaginary and are not intended to refer to specific places or living persons. The opinions expressed in this manuscript are solely the opinions of the author and do not represent the opinions or thoughts of the publisher. The author has represented and warranted full ownership and/or legal right to publish all the materials in this book.

Bobby
A Young Man Claimed by God
All Rights Reserved.
Copyright © 2011 Jean McDowell
v2.0

Cover Photo © 2011 JupiterImages Corporation. All rights reserved - used with permission.

This book may not be reproduced, transmitted, or stored in whole or in part by any means, including graphic, electronic, or mechanical without the express written consent of the publisher except in the case of brief quotations embodied in critical articles and reviews.

Outskirts Press, Inc.
http://www.outskirtspress.com

ISBN: 978-1-4327-7277-2

Outskirts Press and the "OP" logo are trademarks belonging to Outskirts Press, Inc.

PRINTED IN THE UNITED STATES OF AMERICA

# ACKNOWLEDGEMENTS

I wish to dedicate this book to my dear mother, who, in this her nine-tieth year is unable to read, never mind, comprehend, its contents. She is afflicted with the saddest of all conditions, that of the mind. During her life, before the Alzheimer's disease took hold of her, she sought to teach her family the importance of the Bible, and her exam-ple of personal prayer and dedicated church attendance inspired me. The example given to me by both my Mom and Dad helped make me the person I am today. I am so very glad they were my parents.

I want to give my thanks to my daughter, Rachel, son Jonathan, son-in-law, Dexter and my daughter-in-law Elizabeth. I am so blessed to have them for my children. My grandchildren are the most pre-cious people in my life. So, Malachi, Ashley, Dexter Joel, Bailey Jean, Matthew, Gillian, Mackenzie and last but not least, my little Eli (who always makes sure my calls are answered), thank you all for showing your care for me in such a kind and loving way.

My thanks also go to my brother Victor, and my sister Marie, who encouraged me to finish my book, and were the first to read it. Also thanks to the Kiser family for giving me the final push towards publishing.

To my dear husband, thank you, thank you. I am so glad you asked me to marry you. Your unconditional love has made my life worth living.

I will end with my thanks to God for His unconditional love for me, and for the selfless act of giving His only Son, the Lord Jesus Christ, to not only live among men but to die in the place of sinners, so that those who believe in Him might be saved by Grace.

# CHAPTER ONE

The middle child of five children, Bobby found himself responsible for the safety of his two little sisters. His two older brothers had left home three years earlier to escape the wrath of their father. Bobby would like to have gone with them but stayed because Ruthie and Lillian looked to him for peace and security in a home, which afforded them little in the way of either. He was also worried about his mother whom he loved dearly. She loved her children, he knew that, but she was powerless to show any kind of emotion after spending twenty years with a man who derided her every utterance. His father had a routine, which no one interrupted. Bobby and his siblings learned that it was healthier to be seen and not heard in their home. Bobby was seventeen, a good student who loved books and who had found a way to lose himself in them as he grew up in a family ridden by fear.

His father was a very cruel man who was always unhappy about something. There was not a day would go by without some explosion of anger because something or someone did not please his father. Growing up in this environment Bobby realized that his father could not be pleased so he had long since decided that the best thing for him was to stay offside when his father was home. He had watched his sisters try to do little things to make their father happy only to be rebuffed and humiliated by him. Little Ruthie who was six had gathered some blooms on the way home from school one day and put them in a glass. There were no other containers in their home, which could have been used for flowers. When her father came home, she had ceremoniously presented them to him when he sat down at the table. He had swiped them away and hit Ruthie with the glass. She started crying, which inflamed her father even more than usual and he jumped up and lifted his hand to hit her. Thankfully, she ran to her room, followed closely by Bobby who quickly shushed her so as not to encourage their father to come into her room. Their mother had moved quickly also and brought her husband's dinner to the table. Thankfully, the incident ended there and Ruthie was able to subdue her crying and come to the table, and therefore avoid any other interaction with her father that evening. Eventually she had learned that it was better to avoid the attention of her father and stayed as quiet as possible while he was in the home.

Bobby wished things were different but was reluctant to try to change things having seen his brothers come under his father's wrath for daring to question him. He had learned from their '*mistakes*' to stay out of his father's way and do what he was told without question. Many times, he had seen the results of one of his father's tirades when he had gotten out of control and hit his mother. She would almost always have bruises on her face and arms and he knew it was the result of the previous evening's anger. He had for a long time wished that his mother would not make his father angry, but as he grew older, he knew that there was no way she could. She did everything he asked but was never able to please him. He criticized everything she did, her cooking, the way she looked, the way she folded his clothes. He told her often that she could do nothing right.

Bobby resolved that if he ever married he would never treat his wife that way.

He felt sorry for his mother when he saw her black eyes and swollen jaw; would help her when he knew she was in pain and helped her to sweep the floor and carry the laundry. He was careful not to do so when his father was around because he knew better than to draw attention. He was always careful too to never ask his mother if she were okay in front of his father because any attention brought to her bruises and pain, would initiate another scene. She never spoke of the abuse, even in the afternoon when the children would return from school when there was a certain normalcy in their home. Bobby felt like he could actually breathe on those occasions and oftentimes he would hug his mother, and she would tell him that she loved him and that he was a good boy. However, these times were short and there was never much time for small talk or loving embraces because even an hour before his father was due home, his mother would get more and more agitated. She moved about the room, continually fixing his fathers chair and moving the things on the table from here to there trying to remember where her husband wanted them the previous night. He was irritated as he watched her continually trying to please his father, knowing that it was impossible. As the time for his arrival home from work came closer, the two girls would sit close together on the couch, hardly daring to breathe. How he longed to be out of that situation but knew that any action on his part would only incur more hurt for his mother.

He remembered when his brothers had left and decided that he was better off just making sure that his mother and his sisters were safe. His father had beaten his mother for days after they left, yelling obscenities and blaming her because they were gone. His mother would always manage to retreat to their bedroom, even though he followed her there every time. Bobby soon realized that this was her strategy to keep the violence from them. He would usually retreat to his room at that point and make his sisters go to theirs. He often wondered why his mother stayed and did not just run away while his dad was at work, and in fact, for years when he first started school he would worry all day that she would be gone when he came home.

His father would rise in the morning at seven -thirty; eat the breakfast cooked for him by his silent wife, and leave for work at eight-fifteen without having spoken a word. The noise of his pickup leaving the driveway was the signal that they could speak. It was the only time in their lives when their mother talked to them. She would tell them to be good and enjoy school, would present them with some kind of treat that she had secreted for them. Their father did not permit her to spend money on such things but she did it anyway. It was the only rebellion to her husband that Bobby ever witnessed, and he knew it was one way that she could show her love for her children. It made him smile because he knew it was a risk and that she was willing to take it for them.

At six o'clock at night, his father would come home armed with his six-pack of beer, sit down at the table and lift his knife and fork. That was the signal for everyone to jump to attention. His mother would bring his father's plate and then the others, while he complained that it was too hot or too cold, that the food had not been cooked long enough or was over-cooked. They kept their eyes on their plates and ate without comment, trying to pace them so that they would finish at the same time as their father and not incur his anger for eating too fast or too slow. After dinner, they would retreat to their rooms and read until bedtime. If their father would want their doors closed, they could have hushed conversations, but on the occasions when he decided that they were closing the doors to hide something they would continue their dinner silence until bedtime.

School was a relief to them. There was no angry yelling and the teachers all seemed to like their work, and they all excelled. Lillian went to the same school, as Bobby and they would get together for lunch. Bobby was glad of her company, as he did not care much for his classmates. They were always in some kind of stress about trivial things, and he did not care to get involved in their problems. He usually retreated to the library when he had free time and encouraged Lillian to do the same. After school, they would meet up at the front door and walk to the school where Ruthie attended. They had an arrangement where one of the teachers who stayed late after school would allow two and sometimes three children to stay in her room after school until they were picked up. It worked well and their mother was able to avoid being seen with her bruised face. One day the teacher asked him if everything was ok at home. He was taken by surprise but managed to give an evasive answer. The look on his face however prompted the teacher to give him a little more information regarding her question. She said that she was quite worried about the drawings, which Ruthie was presenting to them. Apparently, the teacher gave paper and colored pencils to the children to keep them busy after school. . She had placed them in a folder and asked Bobby to give them to his parents and ask them to come to the school for a visit. Bobby did not give the folder to his mom. He decided that to do so would cause more problems at home so he kept it in his room and when dinner was over, he looked at the pictures. There were ugly scary faces all over her pages. The colors were all purple, red, and black. She had drawn people lying down but their faces were all scratched over. He knew what they were about and felt sorry for Ruthie because they indicated to him that she lived in fear. He thought of telling her teacher, and then decided that to do so would probably mean that there would be more trouble from their father and things were already bad enough. Next day he told the teacher that his mother would be in to see her but that she was busy for the next few days. He hoped that the teacher would forget all about the drawings.

No one ever talked while his father was in the house. Bobby did not really think about it much. He left them alone for the most part, occasionally flinging open their doors yelling about never knowing what was going on in his own house. They were always lying on their beds reading (something Bobby had told the girls to do,) and when their father saw that he would go away. He never went into their rooms and this gave them a sense of security. Their mother made sure that their rooms stayed tidy, not that they had many belongings. Toys and games cost money and their father did not allow money to be spent on such things. They got books from the school library and he looked at them every so often to make sure that they had not purchased them.

They enjoyed walking home together, and sometimes discussed

their home situation. Bobby would encourage them to not worry and tell them what to do to stay out of trouble. He tried to joke with them and often made Ruthie giggle with delight. Lillian was another story. She was so angry so he just let her vent about how unfair life was and how she wished that she had been born in a different family. He felt sorry for his sisters but felt powerless to do anything about their situation. At home, Ruthie would pull the covers over her head to try and close out all the yelling and screaming. She would fall asleep most nights this way, and on others she would sob very quietly and Lillian would climb into bed beside her, and hold her until she fell asleep. She would tell Bobby how scared Ruthie was at night and he in turn would tell Lillian that she was doing the right thing in keeping Ruthie quiet.

One day a classmate of Lillian's asked if she could tag along with them after school. She said that her brother was starting school in September, and she would like to pick him up but did not relish the idea of walking alone. Bobby wanted to say no to her because he liked that they were able to talk about their situation freely on the way home, but this girl, well she looked like what he thought an angel would look like. She was very shy and did not talk much and Bobby was somewhat tongue-tied. He did not know why all of a sudden he did not know what to say. He would look at her often on their way home and would catch her looking at him. He loved the way the sun glinted in her hair; he loved how blue her eyes were. When she did speak, her voice was soft. He was smitten. He resolved that one day he would marry someone who looked like her. They walked home together for the last two weeks of school and by then they were talking and laughing together. Even Lillian seemed happier. Bobby was so sad on the last day of school because he knew that he would not see her again for a few months. By that time, he had already decided that he was going to marry this beautiful girl.

He had never paid much attention to girls. His focus had been to take care of his siblings, so talking to his female classmates had either never occurred to him or was strained. Most of his classmates thought he was an oddball and mostly left him to himself. One or two had tried to pick fights with him but his non-retaliation made them lose interest. The girls would mostly whisper in corners and giggle as he passed by. Anna was different. Talking to her was easy; she had such a sweet nature and was as beautiful inside as she was on the outside. He would say her name to himself as he lay in bed at night. Even her name sounded soft to him. He was in love. She was so perfect He wondered how he would ever get to the point where he could even ask her out on a date. He knew he could never bring her home. He wanted his mom to meet her but knew that was impossible. He had one more thing to worry about. He could not even imagine what his father would have to say about something like that.

Lillian really enjoyed being with the other kids. She seemed to be able to throw off her cloak of anger and always had fun at the park. Lunchtimes were pleasant too. Their mother listened to them as they talked about whom they had met at the park and what they had done. She would smile and tell them she was glad they were happy. The evenings were difficult. Their father always found something to complain about. It made Bobby want to scream when his father would complain about something his mom had done, because the previous night he had yelled at her for not doing it that way. He kept silent, however because that was what his mother had told him to do. She did not want to lose another son. She spoke of Joseph and Thomas sometimes at lunch and wondered where they were and what they were doing. She hoped that maybe they had found their grandparents. She told Bobby that she hoped one day he would be able to find them. She said that they were good people, and she wanted her children to know them.

School ended for the year and the long tedious summer was upon them. The days were not so bad. His mother allowed bobby to take his sisters to the park and they played with the other kids there. He joined with some boys kicking a ball about sometimes, but most of the time he read his books and answered Ruthie's many questions. She seemed more withdrawn and he tried to encourage her to play with the other kids. She was content to sit very close to him on the park bench and ply him with questions about everything. He decided that she really was craving attention so he would spend his time telling her some of the things he had read in his books. She would listen enthralled as he described different animals and their habitats. Every so often she would pose a question like, "Does the daddy bear love his cubs?" Bobby knew that the question in her mind was really, "Does my daddy love me?" That was a question he could not answer.

# CHAPTER TWO

His mother's parents had been involved in a car wreck when she was very young. Her father had been killed instantly, and her mother a few months later from the injuries sustained in the accident. She had gone to live with an aunt who had let her know every day what a burden she was. When she was thirteen, she met their dad and three years later, they got married when she found she was pregnant. His parents were very kind but did not really want their only son to get married so young. They tried to talk sense to him one day and he stormed out and never went back to see them again. When the baby was born, she asked him to take them to see his parents and he flew into a rage. The situation became worse when he found out that she had called their son Joseph after her dad. He had not come to the hospital to see her after he dropped her off and so she filled out all the necessary paperwork herself. She had at one time thought that he was not coming back for her. Her day of discharge arrived and he did not. They had no phone so no one could call him. The nurses were getting ready to call the police when he showed up after work and told her to hurry up and get ready because she needed to go home.

He stayed mad about the name for a long time, and in fact, things were never the same, but for the sake of her little one, she tried to make the best of it. By the time she was twenty she had three sons and she knew that she had made a big mistake marrying this cruel man. Pushing, shoving, and an occasional fist in her face now accompanied the yelling and screaming. Her babies kept her busy and happy during the day when her husband was at work and she accepted life with him because of those intervals. She thanked God that he did work because she was able to love and care for her children, something that irritated her husband, because they took her attention away from him. Joseph Alan, Thomas Ryan and Robert John Swanson were all healthy strong babies and she took great pride in the fact that she had been able to nurse them without him knowing. He had made it very clear that she was to feed the babies *'properly'* so she fed them through the day and pumped enough to last through the nights and Sundays. That was the only day he did not work. When she told him that she was pregnant for the fourth time and that it was a girl, he was so mad he knocked her down and kicked her. She started contracting and lost the baby that night, alone in the bathroom while he snored. The next morning the sight of her lying on the bathroom floor where she had passed out, and the sight of the blood scared him a little, although not enough for him to stay home and help her. She managed to get through the next few days, caring for her babies and herself with no help, scared to go to a doctor or seek any kind of help. The incident brought her great misery but also some respite from the abuse. Her husband did not speak one word to her for the next month but when he started speaking to her things were much worse than before. He accused her of having a miscarriage to get him into trouble. She denied this and he pushed her and made her fall almost on top of one of her boys. She made up her mind then that she would never try to explain herself again. She apologized even though she knew she had done nothing wrong and that became her pattern.

As the years went by she started believing that it was true and that she was to blame and spent her life trying to get things right so that he would be pleased. He never was. When pregnant with Lillian she did not tell him, and when she brought home a baby girl, he beat her because she had delivered a girl, and told her it must be someone else's baby. She was black and blue when he was done and when he saw her he packed up and left. She was at the point where she thought he was not coming back when in he walked, angrier than ever, blaming her for trying to get him into trouble. A pattern developed, He would beat her and leave. A few days later, he would come back and yell and scream at her for trying to get him into trouble. She spent her life apologizing never really understanding what trouble he was talking about. The next seven years brought two more miscarriages because of the abuse, and losing precious lives like that brought its own misery and much heartache. She was so worried about her children and prayed continuously that God would keep them safe in his loving arms. She remembered her mother praying with her at night and saying those words. After Ruth was born, the abuse became a daily routine. The shoving and pushing had by that time escalated to beating and kicking. Thomas, her second son tried to intervene. He could not stand to go to his room and listen to the thuds as his mother quietly took what she now thought was her due. He tried to get between them on more than one occasion and came in contact with his father's fists. A few times his father had turned his attention to him but because he had had too much to drink, he was no match for his son and backed off. When his father was at work, his mother would beg him refrain from interfering with his father's treatment of her. She told him it only made his father angrier. Thomas saw how upset his mother was and tried to stay out of the fights but found it to be very difficult.

When Ruth was four years old, she was so excited about her birthday. They had a cake at lunchtime to avoid any problem with their father. It had butterflies on it and was pink and purple. Her eyes were shining as she blew out the candles with the help of her siblings. At that moment, all was well in the world. Then the unthinkable happened. Their father arrived home early. He had been in a fight at work and had been sent home to think things over. When he arrived, everyone was so surprised that there was no opportunity to hide the cake and he flew into a rage about wasted money and knocked the cake to the floor. Ruthie ran to her cake to rescue her butterflies and her father swiped at her. She was so fast that he missed her but he stomped on her cake narrowly missing her little arm. His wife went to rescue Ruthie and he then knocked his wife to the floor and grabbed her by the hair pushing her face into the smashed cake, screaming about wasting his money. Ruthie started screaming because she was so scared.

Thomas lost his resolve and went over to help his mother up while Lillian grabbed Ruthie and took her to their bedroom. Their father knocked Thomas to the floor and chairs went flying. Their father lifted one of the chairs just as Joseph moved to help Thomas. Joseph received a blow to the head, which dazed him somewhat, and he staggered back behind the table. At this time, his mother was up and ushered him towards the bedroom door signaling to Thomas to go there too. Thomas was nearer to the front door and went out there. Their father went and locked the door and lay down on the couch where he slept for the night, so no-one would be able to let Thomas back in. He spent the night lying out on the concrete path because their mother was so afraid of invoking more violence by allowing him in. She slept very little that night afraid of what would happen in the morning.

Next morning after their dad went to work Joseph let Thomas in, packed a plastic bag with all their clothes, said their goodbyes to their mother, who tearfully begged them not to go. Joseph was determined, and told his mother they needed to go before one of them killed the brute. She hugged them, and while they said, their sad farewell to their siblings went and brought them an envelope. In it was a few hundred dollars, which she had scrimped and saved. She begged them to be careful and not get into trouble. She asked Joseph to look after Thomas who was only sixteen and told them to try to find their grandparents and gave them a general idea of where she thought they lived. She was particularly worried about Thomas who did not have the sense yet to stay out of fights. She trusted Joseph because she knew he had a level head on his shoulders and could take care of himself. She loved them both but had a soft spot for Thomas because he had always tried to help her, but she also knew that it could be his undoing if he stayed with her.

She hugged them and let them go not realizing that she was looking at them for the last time.

Their mother, anticipating their father's anger when he would come home from work, fed her children early and sent them to their rooms and closed the doors. After Ruthie's third attempt to leave, and be near her mother, she asked Bobby to stay in the room with the girls. He did this gladly knowing that it would give him a much-needed task to focus on when his father returned home. He encouraged them to read books. There was precious little reading actually done. They just sat in position and waited. His mother told him that the boys were gone, that they had left that morning. The expected anger was just as expected with much shouting and yelling about it being her fault that the boys were gone, and questioning as to why she had not stopped them. He left for a week after that and life was calm. When he returned he was livid, told her that she had made the boys leave to get him into trouble, shoved her, and hit her as she retreated to their bedroom. That was followed by the usual thuds as he punched and hit her. Bobby so wished he could make it all stop. After the brothers left, Ruthie became very clingy following her mother around as if she was afraid that she would leave too and Bobby tried his best to entertain her, so she would leave their mother alone in the evenings and not to bring on the violence any sooner than usual.

The next few years were ugly for everyone in the home. Bobby's heart ached for their mother but felt weak and powerless. When the time came for Ruthie to start school, he talked to her often about it, trying to prepare her for the separation from her mother. Her first day of school was traumatic. She was terrified about leaving her mother. That morning she went with Bobby and he stayed with her until the teacher was able to get her settled, and she stopped crying. She settled in pretty well and seemed to enjoy her time there, and never cried again about going to school. He took care of all the papers that were sent home making sure everything was signed well before their father's homecoming.

They did not talk about school when their dad was home. In fact, they did not talk at all when their father was home. The evenings were nervously quiet except for the loud bellowing of their father.

Lillian enjoyed school in a limited way. She could not open up to anyone because she was so ashamed of her home situation. Their parents never showed up for anything and their teachers sent home note after note. There was never any response because their parents never received the notes, except those from Ruthie's teacher. Bobby would be given anything, which needed her parent's attention, and if there was time before his father came home he would have his mother read and sign. If not he would take care of it himself. Her teachers never knew that there was a problem. She skipped and jumped on the way home until they came within sight of their home and then like clockwork, all three of them would go into silent mode. Lillian was quite talkative at first and told Bobby how much she wished they did not have to go home. She would deride her mother's prayers to Bobby and he would quietly tell her that prayer was what kept their mother from going insane. He truly did not understand why, he just knew that he had caught her on numerous occasions kneeling by her bed asking for help for each of her children by name and once when he had heard her praying and telling God that her son Bobby was special and to please take care of him and help him grow up to be a godly young man, he was strangely awed. He told Lillian that the reason she prayed was because she did not know what else to do. Lillian gave up complaining about her mother and decided that Bobby was unsympathetic to her feelings, but she resolved in her heart that if ever she had the chance she would leave their home and never come back. She really did not believe Bobby when he would tell them, that one day, when he was old enough; they would all leave, and go far away, where their father would not find them.

# CHAPTER THREE

Bobby's life had changed since meeting Anna. He cherished the short time he spent with her each day. She brightened his whole day and made his life seem worth living. He looked forward to the day when he was no longer responsible for his sisters and mother and he could spend more time with her. He dreamed of her at night and looked forward each day to the walk home. They talked about everything, except his home. He was too ashamed to tell her of that. He thought it would be nice to have some money so he could buy her something. He asked his mother if he could go and look for a job. His mother reminded him what had happened when Joseph had gotten a job and his father had made him give it up. Bobby was disappointed. Then his mother surprised him by saying that if it was just on Saturday and Sunday and he was home before his father, it would probably be ok. She begged him to be careful that his father would not find out. He thought that after he had bought something for Anna he would save the rest of his money and when he had enough he would take his mother and sisters and find somewhere else to live. The thought gave him so much delight that he walked into the first store he came to, a little hardware store he passed every day on the way home from school. The owner knew him because he had occasionally gone there to get things for his mother. He asked the owner if he could use some help because he needed a job. The owner, Mr. Weldon, told him that he did not need any help at the weekend because his own son helped out, but that he could use some help after school. Bobby told him that he had to be home before six, actually ten minutes before six. Mr. Weldon was slightly amused thinking that Bobby was thinking only of his stomach, but he told him that it would work out perfectly, because the store closed at five-thirty. Bobby was ecstatic. He raced home to tell his mother and she seemed pleased. She encouraged him to open a bank account when he was paid and to save. He did not know what was in her mind but he told her what was in his. She cried a little but told him that he made her happy, so he was very pleased with himself.

Mr. Weldon was a kind man and very patient. He invited Bobby to work through the school break Bobby told him that he could work some days but he would always have to leave at five forty-five. His boss could tell that this was important to him so he agreed that even if they stayed open late Bobby could leave at the appointed time. Bobby enjoyed his time at the store. Mr. Weldon taught him where everything went and gave him the job of putting the new supplies away each day. Bobby had the job done in no time. He took it upon himself to generally clean up, put out the trash and tidy the store at the end of each day. His boss was impressed and knew that he had found a gem. The owner played gospel music in his store and before long Bobby found himself humming along. He was surprised at himself because music had never been a part of his life. Mr. Weldon heard him humming and gave him a CD, which had some of the songs that he played in the store. Bobby thanked him very much. He had never owned anything so shiny and new before. However, he had no way to play it. And even if he had he could never play it at home. He put it safely away resolving to play music when he was able to find a new home for his mom and sisters.

One day he was busy stacking a new delivery of washers and screws when he heard a familiar voice. It was his angel. She was there with her parents and her brother. He looked at them with a tinge of jealousy. They were all so happy. Her dad had his arm around her and she was showing him a door pull, which she thought she would like for her room. She caught sight of him and quickly introduced him to her parents who thanked him profusely for walking her home from school each day. He was surprised that they knew that because Anna just said that this was Bobby. He told himself that he knew she came from a family like that. He saw her dad several times in the next few months when he would come to the store. He always sought Bobby out and shook his hand. Bobby would think to himself how nice it was to be normal.

Every day after school when he walked Anna home he felt happy that she was going home to a happy home and wished he could provide the same for his family. By now, he had realized that his dream was along way off but his resolve never wavered. His life seemed to move faster as he looked forward to seeing her each day. Lillian started walking on ahead jealous of the way conversation came so easy to Bobby and Anna. She was becoming very bitter about her situation and did not really believe that Bobby would be able to do anything to help them. She was also a little jealous of Anna because Bobby had told her of his meeting with her parents. The school year went in way too fast and now they were walking home again for the last day of the year. He told her that he hoped she would come into the store with her father sometimes and she said she would. When they parted, she squeezed his hand and her touch nearly drove him crazy. He wanted to kiss her. He was mortified at the thought. He made up his mind that next year he would ask her if he could hold her hand on the way home from school. The thought made him smile as he walked into the hardware store. Mr. Weldon saw that smile and commented that he must be very happy that day. Bobby nodded. He was hopelessly in love.

One day Bobby was in the middle of stacking when he suddenly saw that it was time to go He jumped up and started to say that he still needed to leave but Mr. Weldon said it for him and laughed. "Is that because dinner is on the table at home?" He asked. Bobby, who had grown to trust his boss, answered quickly "No it's because my dad comes home and he can't find out that I am working, or my mom will catch it" "Oh!" was the answer and Bobby knew he had said too much. He quickly took off leaving Mr. Weldon with a question on his lips.

Sensing that Bobby did not want to discuss the subject farther he let it drop and never brought it up again. Home continued with the same monotonous evenings dotted with his father's predictable tirades. Lillian was becoming more and more sullen and Ruthie did not like to spend the evenings with her so she more often that not would find her way into Bobby's room he could read her stories. She loved her big brother and often fell asleep on the end of his bed. He would quietly carry her to her own bed and tuck her in, say a goodnight to Lillian, who had started rudely ignoring him. He understood her anger and did not ever retaliate. He would lie awake and wish for the next day. He had realized what it was like to be out in the world as he thought and he rather liked it. His little bank account was steadily growing, simply because he has no reason to spend anything. Every week he would tell his mother how much they had and receive a hug from her. He rose early in the morning, got himself ready for work and waited until he heard his father's truck leave the driveway and then kiss his mother and run to work.

The store was to be closed on July 4th, so the day before was busy. His boss had put him in charge of sales while he made some phone calls. Bobby felt elated. This was a position of trust and he was thrilled that his boss thought that he was trustworthy. He stood there and within a few minutes, there was a line. He did what he was supposed to do having watched his boss go through the transactions. He was very patient with customers asking questions and methodically took care of each customer. His boss had finished his phone call and was about to come and rescue him when he saw the smiling customers leaving. One even came over to him on the way out to say what a nice person Bobby was. He agreed with them wholeheartedly. He decided to leave Bobby at the counter and go and take care of some much-needed paperwork. It was another hour before he came back to check on Bobby. He was in his element, explaining things to customers; climbing up to get high items and writing down orders for things that were not in stock. His boss grinned. He had not been wrong about this guy. He was a natural…and he seemed to love people as much as they loved him. He would have to try to hold unto him. If only he knew what made him tick. He still wondered about the reason, he was so anxious about being home on time.

Later on in the afternoon Anna's father appeared, and seemed genuinely happy to see him in his new job. He wanted something to strengthen an awning he had put up in his yard for the next day. Bobby found him something, which perfectly suited his needs, and He was very grateful. He so wished that he had brought Anna with him. Before he left he said something which sent Bobby's heart soaring. He invited him and his family over for the festivities the following day. "Oh," he thought, "God has heard my prayers." How he wished he could go. Maybe his dad would be working and his mom could come. He thanked Anna's dad and said he would certainly try. Anna's dad then put his arm around him and said, "You're a good kid". Wow! That was praise indeed from someone who didn't really know anything about him. He floated through the rest of the day and just before he left, his boss shook his hand and said that he had done so well that he was going to give him a raise.

He ran home so that he would have time to ask his mom if they could go. She saw the glow and knew instinctively, as only a mother can, that Anna must be very important to him. She did not promise, but said that if their dad was working the next day, she would make some pies for him to take. He was thrilled. He told his sisters and for once Lillian seemed excited. Ruthie, who loved Anna as much as Bobby did, was beside herself with excitement. There was to be a barbeque, games, and everything. This was going to be a great day. However, everything depended on their dad's plans for the next day, and they all wondered what would happen.

He came home in a foul mood. The store had been sold out of his beer. Someone had cut him off on the way home. He had to work tomorrow. On and on went his complaints, but they never heard another word. He was working…tomorrow. They were holding their breath. Their mother, not wanting their father to see their reaction to his news, kept apologizing to him as if everything that had happened to him that day was her fault. That seemed to annoy him even more and he shoved the table into her stomach and knocked everything off the table unto the floor. That was the cue for the children to make themselves scarce and at Bobby's silent command they went to their rooms. He only needed to look at them and then look at their room door and off they would go. He slowly moved towards his own room even though he really wanted to protect his mother. Their father ranted and raved and they heard their mother groan as he hurt her in some way. Ruthie climbed unto Lillian's bed and her sister held the shaking child close. Poor little Ruthie was trembling and Lillian could do nothing less than allow her to stay close to her while the noise continued. How she wished she could just become someone else.

Meantime Bobby closed his ears to the noise. He tried to drown out the racket by thinking of Anna, and of seeing her next day. He tried to close his mind to the violence outside his door. He wished his older brothers would come back and finish that brute off. He wanted to kill him, he hated him so. He made up his mind that in the morning he would try to persuade his mom to leave. He would tell her about his raise and ask his boss to help find a place for them. He so wanted to go out there and knock some sense into his dad but he kept his place as his mother had requested. It seemed to take forever to end, but it finally did and he slept soundly dreaming sweet dreams of angels and Anna and new homes and peace. He woke up next morning and found the sun streaming in the window, Ruthie sleeping at the end of his bed, and Lillian lying on the floor with her pillow and a blanket from her bed. He knew that the tirade must have continued for a long time for Lillian to come to his room as well.

He heard his father growling at his mother because his breakfast did not please him. Then he heard sounds of more furniture being thrown around the room. He stayed very still not wanting his father to have any reason to open his door and find the girls. He finally heard the truck pull out and up he got. He went to check on his mother. She was still in her bedroom so he showered and dressed letting the girls sleep. His mother still did not come out so when the girls woke up he made them breakfast and they sat at the table silently eating, wondering what they should do. This had never happened before and Bobby was visibly uneasy. Lillian asked him what they should do but he did not know. They were still sitting there when her door opened and all three of them gasped when they say her face. It was bruised and bleeding. Bobby knew at once that she would not go to the picnic, not looking like that. One of her eyes was closed shut, and she looked grotesque, not like herself at all. He went over to her and gently put his arm around her and said "Mom we have got to get out of here. He is going to kill you. I got a raise. We can find somewhere else to live. You have to come. He was sobbing by this time. Lillian was crying too and holding her sad, frightened little sister with both arms.

His mother told him that she would be all right, that she would lie down for a while and then later bake the pies for them. He did not care about pies. He wanted to carry his mother to safety. He begged her to pack some things and leave. He told her he knew where his boss lived and that he would help find them somewhere to stay. She still maintained that she was fine, that it was just a bit of swelling and that it would be fine. She told them that they should go and not worry about her. She finally persuaded the girls to stop crying and they washed up the dishes for her. She uncharacteristically kissed them and Bobby. She told him that he was a good boy. She said that in a little while she would bake their pies and that they should go and have a wonderful day. Then she told them all that she loved them and she lay down and soon was sleeping peacefully.

Bobby let her sleep. He figured that she must be really tired. He had never known his mother to sleep during the day. So he did not wake her up. He kissed her and when she slept on, he took the two girls and left without the pies. He bought a watermelon and some fruit at the little fruit stand and took those along. Anna's mother was so glad to see them, thanked them for the fruit and took it into the kitchen. She seemed genuinely sorry that their mother could not come, and said that maybe next time she would be able. Bobby thought of asking her if she could help them find somewhere for them to live but decided to wait till later. Maybe he could slip home and get his mother and they could see that they really needed help.

He played basketball with Anna's dad and a couple of boys he had seen at school. Their dads were there and Anna's little brother. They all had such a great time. Anna took the girls to her room where she told Ruthie to choose some dolls to play with. Ruthie thought she was in heaven. She had never seen such a pretty room with so many things to play with. They stayed there for a while then went outside to the pool. Anna had found a couple of suits that she had grown out of and they fitted the girls perfectly, and they were overjoyed. They had never owned a swimsuit, much less played in a pool. Ruthie was a little afraid at first but soon found that her feet touched the bottom and she had the best of times. They splashed around for most of the day, eating and drinking whenever they felt like it. It was so different to their regimented life. They had no idea life could be so grand. Bobby caught sight of them every so often and smiled inwardly. I know I can make them happy, he thought. All he needed was to persuade his mom to leave today.

He told Lillian his plans and they decided to go home earlier than necessary so they would have time to pack. It had been a long time since he has seen Lillian so animated about anything. He told Anna's mother that they were going home and she tried to persuade them to stay. We have lights strung up and fireworks. Bobby said that they would go and get their mom and come back. He knew that his mother's eyes would light up when she saw the fireworks and she would be so happy to know she didn't have to go back. Before they left Bobby told Anna's dad what he was planning and asked him if he could help them find a place. He was appalled and wanted to call the police but when he saw the alarm in Bobby's eyes he told them that they could all stay with them for a while until they found a place. He would discuss it with his wife. Off the three of them ran. They were so excited. Anna's dad gathered his family together and they prayed for Bobby and his family. None of them had realized that anything like this was going on. They decided to wait till Bobby came back with his mother, before doing anything drastic. They knew something had to be done, but what. They would stay with them of course until things got settled. They waited and talked quietly completely forgetting the fireworks. Anna's father thought he might go and see if he could help, maybe pack some things but his wife cautioned him and said that Bobby was a very sensible boy and would know what to do. He would ask for help if they needed it. So they continued to wait and wonder. Anna helped her mother prepare the room for the girls and the couch in the family room for Bobby.

# CHAPTER FOUR

Bobby and his sister set out from the party with bated breath. Bobby was glad that he had made the decision to leave. Lilly was so excited she could hardly contain herself, and Ruthie skipped along gaily because Bobby had told her that they were going to get their Mom and bring her to the party. As they turned the corner of their street they all saw it at the same time.........their father's truck. Bobby groaned audibly. Now what! They hoped that their mother was awake before he got home. Why was he home so soon? How were they going to get their mother out now? What reason were they going to give as to where they were? Bobby was in a dilemma. They were almost free. He decided that they would go home anyway. Maybe their father would leave again, go back to work. Maybe he was just home for food. Maybe he forgot his lunch. Although they had no desire to see him, their steps became more hurried. They went in through the back door. The television, which was on continually while their father was home, was silent. The house was unusually quiet. Their mother was asleep on the couch. Their father appeared out of their bedroom with a bag of his clothes, barked at them to pack because they were leaving. This was so screwed up. They were not supposed to go with him. They were supposed to be leaving him behind. It was surreal. His father went back to the bedroom and was feverishly picking up stuff and shoving it into another bag. Bobby went to wake his mom up and soon realized that she was not breathing. He told the girls to go to their room and he ran next door to call an ambulance. His neighbor told him that he would do that for him and he ran back to the house just in time to see his father dragging Lillian to his pick-up. Ruthie was already inside sobbing in fear. Bobby ran to the door and grabbed Ruthie out just as Lillian broke free. There was no way that he was going to let his dad take her. He grabbed at Lilly, swore when he missed her and came after them, changed his mind and jumped in and drove out of the driveway taking part of the hedge with him. The neighbor came out just then and asked if the girls wanted to go with her.

The ambulance was there before they could collect their wits, and the paramedics ran inside asking questions as they moved. What happened? When did she stop breathing? Had this ever happened before? They stopped abruptly when they saw their mother. Who did this? Bobby was sick when they looked at him. They thought he had done it. He kept silent when they asked him if he knew who the perpetrator was, fearing his father's return. They would be at his mercy if they told on him and he found out. They quickly examined their mother and shook their heads. She was gone. "No! No!" Bobby groaned when the news sank in. He had waited too long. He sank down on his knees and sobbed. The paramedics called the police before moving his mother. They were there in minutes, questioning Bobby, Lillian and Ruthie. They wrote some things down and then made some calls. They were taking pictures. All the flashing made him dizzy. Everything was spinning out of control and he was powerless to stop it. Before long people arrived and told the children they were social workers. They separated the three children and questioned them.

He finally told them about the beatings. When they were all satisfied that their stories were the same they called for more police. Soon yellow tape surrounded their home. Neighbors were out in the street trying to find out what was wrong. Ruthie was white and trembling. Bobby felt that it was all his fault that his mother was dead. If only he hadn't left her. If only he had made her leave 24 hours ago. "If only." He moaned to himself in his anguish and confused the officers who were standing around. They asked him again if he had hurt his mother and he cried and said that he was going to save her today and get her away from his father and all the beatings. They felt sorry for the boy, and were genuinely moved by his distress. He told them that he needed to take his sisters back to Anna's parents' home because he was afraid that they wouldn't be safe at home. One of them patted him on the back and said, that they were all going to a safe place and he need not worry any more.

They were taken to a large building at the other side of the city, where they were separated once more. Ruthie and Lillian were given separate rooms. Bobby tried to tell them that she would be scared and needed to be with her sister or him. He asked if he could see her, and after some deliberation they agreed. When he walked into the room she threw herself at him and was trembling with fear. Bobby held her tight and told her that everything would be all right. He told her not to be afraid and to try and sleep and then in the morning they would try to find somewhere else to live and they would be happy. He had no idea what was in store for him in the morning. She kept asking where her mom was and when she could see her, when she was going home. Bobby was struggling to hold himself together for his sisters but she was so terrified that once or twice he almost lost it and broke down. He managed to hold it together until he was shown to his room then he broke down and sobbed till he thought his heart would break.

Anna's family realized that Bobby was not coming back and they were afraid for the kids. They also realized that they didn't even know where exactly Bobby lived. They waited for a while then her dad called Mr. Weldon. He was not home. Later he called the police and was told that the children were all safe and were being taken care off. He was satisfied that everything was okay and told his family not to worry. He was sure that Bobby would be in touch with him in the morning. However he slept fitfully wondering why the police were involved and what they meant. He wondered what had happened and had a very bad feeling but kept his thoughts to himself.

Next day he heard all about the tragedy on the news and felt over-whelming sadness for Bobby and his sisters. He called the police for news of the children but got none. He called into the hardware store and found that Bobby had not shown up for work that day and Mr. Weldon had no idea why until he told him about what had happened the previous day. They went into the office and prayed together for the family. Anna did not hear the news, so she was very perturbed when she didn't hear from Bobby. She kept asking her mother and then later her father. Finally her parents sat down with her and told her the sad story. She had so many questions, but they did not have any answers. Her heart was so burdened for Bobby. She loved him so much.

# CHAPTER FIVE

After a long night of turmoil and fitful sleep, Bobby awoke to a new day. Things would be better he thought, they certainly couldn't get worse. But they did. The two girls were taken to two different foster homes. They would be well taken care of and would be safe. He told them over and over that they would be safe with him and that someone was going to help them find a place to stay. He knew the address but no telephone number. There was no-one there willing to go check it out. He told them that he had friends who would let them stay at their home. The workers discussed all of his information and decided that these friends should have taken care of this situation long ago. They couldn't risk the safety of the children. The consensus was that they were better off in foster care. They did not tell Bobby why that decision was made only that it was made. He was in so much distress. He felt like the ground was slipping away from under him. He looked out the window and saw his precious Ruthie being dragged into a car. She looked petrified. He waved but she could not see him. The workers would not tell him where she going to stay. They kept telling him it was for their own good.

He didn't know where to turn; no one was listening to him. He had lost his whole family. He didn't know where his brothers were. They would know what to do. He had promised his mother that he would look after his sisters and they were gone. They didn't even have each other. He felt as if he was sinking beneath the waves and did not have the strength to pull himself up. He tried going through the hallways looking for Lillian but could not find her. He was reprimanded for being in the wrong area. He found some offices but they were all locked. He was frantic. He sat down on a bench when he was satisfied that he had looked everywhere. That was where the workers found him. He was reprimanded again because they thought that he had run off. He was told that he could not leave the building until the investigation of his mother's death was finished. They told him that they could not find his father, and it was too dangerous for him to be out there wandering around. He asked them if he could go home to shower and change. He was given a box of clothes someone had picked up from his room. They said that he could not go home because it was a crime scene and no-one was allowed in. He was told that they were looking for a foster home to place him and they needed his birthday and social security etc. They encouraged him to be patient.

Patient.......... In one fell swoop he had lost his parents, and his sisters, he didn't know where his brothers were and he was to be patient. He felt very alone. He told them that he had a job and needed to there. They told him that they had funds to supply all his needs so he wouldn't need the job right then. The police came again and asked him more questions. Why had he not reported the abuse? He asked himself the same question; he guessed that he didn't know he could. He felt so responsible, so guilty. He remembered his mother's prayers. He didn't feel very special. They told him that they would need him to testify against his dad when he came to trial. He was starting to get angry. At that moment he hated his dad more than anything else in the world. He had been left in the office while discussions about him were taking place in another room. He just flipped. He started knocking things around, and making a lot of noise. He started yelling at the top of his voice that he was not like his father; that his father was a monster, that he loved his mother. He was out of control and did not have the strength to fight that pent-up anger. He yelled at his father and told him that he hated him, that he would kill him if he got the chance. The workers, who didn't seem to know what to do with him called for security and before he understood what was happening he found himself locked in the room. He suddenly saw his father in himself. He was crying again. He was nothing like his father. He would never be like his father. He was now terrified himself. He was locked up, and couldn't escape. He put everything back the way it was before and sat down to wait and see what would happen to him. After what seemed like an eternity someone opened the door. A policeman and a social worker were there. The social worker introduced himself and the officer and asked Bobby if they could sit down and talk with him. A quick look around the room told the worker that the supposed wrecking of the room was a figment of someone's imagination. He looked at the young man and saw pain. He decided to take this case himself. He talked to Bobby for a few minutes and then told the officer that he could handle the situation and they were left alone. He asked Bobby to accompany him to his office, which was closer to where Bobby had slept the night before. He told Bobby that he wanted to hear the whole story and that he had all day so he could take as much time as he needed. At last someone was going to listen to him. He followed the worker and as they passed another office he heard someone say. "We can't put him anywhere with younger siblings. He may have inherited his father's violent tendencies". His restraint threatened to dissolve again. He felt the anger rising in his throat. He wanted to scream at them "I am not like my father". He felt a hand on his shoulder. He was about to run into that room and tear it up and beat those people up for daring to say that he was like his father, but before he had the chance the worker who had introduced himself as Mr. Maddox poked his head through the door and told the somewhat embarrassed group that they should be more careful about what they said when the door was open. He then told them that were all off the hook that he was taking the case and that everything was under control. Then he guided Bobby to his office, offered him some coffee and a doughnut and settled down to listen after placing his phone on silence. Bobby felt the surge of anger die down again as he ate the doughnut. He thanked Mr. Maddox for taking the time to listen and said Mr. Maddox three times in the sentence. Mr. Maddox stopped him and told him that everyone just called him Maddox and he should too. Then he casually asked about his grandparents because one of the children had mentioned them. Bobby told Maddox that he had never met them, that they were his father's parents, and that his mother had wanted someday to have her children meet them but didn't know where they were or how to find them. He told his new friend how he had worked to try and earn enough money so that he could take his mother and sisters to a safe place to live. He found a very sympathetic listener in Maddox. He told how he made sure that his sisters were safe in their rooms when the beatings were taking place and how he wanted to go out and kill his father. He said that he had not because his mother had begged him not to get involved. He talked about his brothers and how he wished he could find them. It was a long day. After several hours Maddox ordered some Pizza, and they ate and then continued talking. It was such a relief to be able at last to tell all. He had hidden it all his life, was always afraid that someone would find out, and that people would look at him in a strange way if they knew. At the end of the day Bobby was exhausted. Maddox told him that because of the circumstances, and because he was a minor he would not be given custody of his sisters. He was sympathetic but told Bobby that they might be upset for a while but that their lives would be so much better without all the violence.

Bobby had to agree. He wasn't happy but he understood there was no other way and he did want the best for his sisters. He was told that they could not find a placement for him because of his age. But that he was welcome to stay at the halls until he finished school. Meantime they would still look for a home, which would welcome him. Maddox managed to secure the rest of the things in his room at home, and they were all at his bedside in the room, which was to be his for a while. Maddox also agreed to get a message to Mr. Weldon so he would know why Bobby had not shown up for work. After visiting the hardware store and talking to his boss, Maddox agreed to drive him to work each day. Bobby was very grateful.

When he arrived at the store Mr. Weldon was very emotional and told Bobby that he was so sorry about all that had happened. He welcomed him back and invited him to eat lunch with him and his wife. Bobby was really glad of the invite and readily agreed. When they sat down to eat Mr. Weldon bowed his head and thanked God for the food and for the fact that Bobby was back. He became very choked up during his prayer and when Bobby opened his eyes Mrs. Weldon was patting her husband on the arm and smiling. Back at the halls, there were no other full time inmates. A worker stayed in the halls each night but Bobby liked those nights best when Maddox was there.

His life took on some kind of normalcy. Bobby decided to make the best of it. He was still saving his money and believed that someday when he was not a minor anymore he would get his sisters and take care of them. Maddox drove him to work every day and someone would pick him up. When school started they drove him to school. He thought that he would like to be a little more independent, so one day he asked Maddox if he would drive him to a store to find out how much a bicycle would cost. Maddox asked him what he needed a bicycle for and when he told him, he said that he would do better than that. He made a phone call, then drove to a house not far from the school and appeared with a shiny blue bicycle. He told Bobby that it had just been donated and was now his. He felt liberated as he rode around on his new wheels. It was so much fun that he decided that he would buy one for each of his sisters once they were all together.

September came and school started. It was good to be back. All his reading through the summer paid off and he aced his first big English test. This really made him very happy. He had always been pretty good at math but he hadn't scored very high in English until now. History was his favorite subject and he always borrowed a history book each time he visited the library. He felt good. He was beginning to feel as if it was worthwhile to be alive. He started to actually believe that there was a God. Mr. Weldon and his wife certainly believed that fact.

Once he was going to the Gym and the girl's tennis club members walked past. Girls being girls they giggled and looked dreamily at him. He was about to disappear quickly when he realized that one of them was Lilly. He was so happy to see her. He grabbed her and told her so. She looked great, with a different hairstyle and new clothes, and looked really pretty. She hugged him back at first then realized that the rest of her friends were watching so she backed up and said that she had to go. He saw her sister occasionally and would stop and say hello. She told him that she was now calling herself Lillian and he was to stop calling her Lilly. She did ask him if he had heard from Ruthie so he knew that deep down she still cared. She told him that she was with a family who had a girl of eleven and a boy who was nine, and that she was very happy. Bobby was satisfied and his thoughts turned to little Ruthie. He hoped that she was as happy as Lillian. He saw Lillian one day and tried to tell her of his plans but she said she had to go. She looked so different. Her hair was cut and styled and her clothes were very different from the ones she used to wear. She seemed to have lots of friends. He tried every day to talk to her and would hang around looking for her. A few times he thought he saw her but couldn't catch up to her. He had the distinct impression that she was deliberately avoiding him. One day he turned a corner and there she was alone for once. He grabbed her and told her how much he missed her. She was very cold and told him that she had a new life and didn't want to be reminded of her old one. He was very hurt but he told her that he would always love her and if she changed her mind he was there. He tried to understand where she was coming from and tried to under-stand her point of view.

He felt lonely for a while after that until one day when locking his bicycle up at the front of the school and he heard a sweet voice saying his name. His beloved Anna was standing there. He was so thrilled that he couldn't find the words to say. She spoke for him. She told him that she had gone with her mother to visit her grandmother who was very ill and had not been back in time to start school. She had just returned at the end of the previous week and this was her first day back. She wanted to know what had happened the night he disappeared. He had so much to tell her, and he only had a few minutes. She asked him if he would walk to the other school with her each day and he was extremely happy to do just that.

That very day he asked Mr. Weldon if he could come to work a few minutes later so that he could walk Anna home. Mr. Weldon winked and told him to take as long as he needed. He told his wife about Anna and she was so excited and told him that she had met Anna and thought that she was a very sweet girl. She had started giving Bobby an extra little treat to take back with him to the halls. She was so sweet, soft-spoken like his mother and obviously very much loved by her husband. He thoroughly enjoyed their lunchtime rendezvous. They talked about their son who had just graduated from the same school. He was away at college and they spoke of him with such pride. He had met him when he first started working at the store. Mrs. Weldon asked one day if he enjoyed working there. He told her that he did and that one day he would like to open a store of his own. He had such dreams. Would any of them unfold? His resolve never wavered... He saved most of the money he earned and that was helped by the fact that Mr. Weldon invited him to eat lunch with him. His wife made the best food. He decided that next to his mother she was the best cook.

His boss did something unusual, before eating his food each day; he bowed his head and thanked God for the food and all the blessings, which had been given him by God. One day he thanked God for bringing Bobby to his store and for the joy that had brought him. Bobby grew to love that man and his wife and one day he used some of his precious money to buy a card for her. She was touched by his thoughtfulness, and told her husband to invite him for supper on

Saturday. He was invited the next week and thereafter it became his routine. It certainly broke the monotony of the halls.

Bobby though about Anna often and hoped that one day she would love him as much as he loved her. All their family secrets were widely published in the newspapers and on the TV. They had not ever been able to watch television in their home, (his dad was the only one who could watch it) and now he did not want to watch it because he was afraid that he would hear more about his family. He thought that her parents would probably tell her to stay away from him. He enjoyed their time together but did not dare tell her what was on his mind, that one day he would ask her to marry him. Yet he dared to dream.

# CHAPTER SIX

Christmas break had arrived and there were a few more people at the halls. He was able to help out quite lot with younger boys. There was always someone who needed help with his or her homework and he was glad to help. He liked that. It made him feel useful. All in all life was not too bad anymore. He still had days when sadness threatened to overwhelm him but he tried to keep busy and always managed to focus again. Maddox checked in with him from time to time and they would spend the entire evening talking if bobby felt like it. Maddox liked the young man and felt like he would make an important contribution to the community one day. He believed that Bobby's experiences had made him strong yet compassionate and those were good traits. He had great hopes for him and tried to encourage him when he could.

At night he would continue to dream. He figured out that by the time he left school he would be eighteen, and he would have enough money to rent somewhere to live, then he would get Ruthie and Lillian and they could all be together again. He was sure that Lillian would warm up to him again once he found Ruthie. He thought about furniture and that was a hindrance to his dreams, but not a deterrent. He was getting along without much money so he naïvely thought that they could too. He went as far as to talk to a lawyer one day to see how much it would cost for a custody hearing. When he heard the estimate he was truly dismayed. He made an appointment to talk to the director of Holman House to find out how difficult it would be to get Ruthie back. He was told that Ruthie had been difficult to place. They figured that she had suffered irreparable harm because of the abuse she had witnessed and suppressed. They thought that she would need to be in care for a long time. As far as they knew a childless couple has taken her under their wing and the last they had heard Ruthie was content and happy. He was sad yet happy for her. He felt that he had let his mother down. He knew that she would have wanted them all to stay together

Lillian didn't seem to want to have anything to do with him although he truly believed that if he was ever able to find Ruthie that she might change her mind. He was able to talk to Mrs. Weldon about this sort of thing. He felt she understood, being a mother. Saturday dinners made some of the happiest memories for him and he loved spending time with them. He helped his boss fix things in the yard and greatly enjoyed his wife's cooking. He helped them to do some painting in the bedroom he presumed was Ricky's. As he left one night Mrs. Weldon asked him what he was planning to do for Christmas, and he told her that he had no specific plans. He said that if there were any other kids in the halls for Christmas they would probably have Christmas dinner for them. She asked him if it would be turkey and all the trimmings and he told her that it would be a first if they had. They usually ordered in food for dinners, there being no specific cook. They had never celebrated Christmas at home because his father would not have approved of the extra cost. She said nothing and Bobby was disappointed because he thought that she might have invited him. He realized that their son was coming home for the holidays and they may want to spend their time with him. He was so grateful for their friendship that he would not allow himself to stay gloomy. He told himself that he had much to be thankful for and he should never take anyone's generosity for granted.

One night that week, he had an unexpected visit from Maddox. He said that he had great news. Bobby thought he had found Ruthie and became excited. However, Maddox told him that it was not that but something else. He sat down and gave him the news that a family had been found who was willing to give him a home until he felt able to step out on his own. He had wished so hard for this at the beginning but when nothing materialized he had actually become quite accustomed to staying here. He was worried that he would have to give up working at the store and he would so miss his Saturday visits with the Weldons. He agreed to meet with the folks but decided that he would not give them an answer until he had talked to his dear friends. He told this to Maddox who thought that was a good idea.

He then walked with him to the main office and when he walked in, he was surprised to see the Weldons already there. "How did you know I needed you?" he asked. With tears in her eyes, Mrs. Weldon said. "It is not you who need us but we who need you." He was totally confused but looked around to see this family who wanted to take him in. He looked at Maddox in bewilderment and he had such a puzzled look on his face Maddox started to laugh. That puzzled him even more when in walked their son. "So you want to be my brother, buddy? Everyone was laughing now at Bobby. It took a few more seconds for it to sink in. "You mean you are the family who wants to take me in?" They all grinned. "You worry too much son," said Maddox. Bobby was so overwhelmed that his eyes filled with tears, tears of absolute joy. They told him to go pick up his stuff because they were not taking no for an answer. Ricky Weldon gave him a push towards the door. "Come on Bro" he teased. "You are so slow to catch on" Off they ran and were soon back, with all his belongings in tow. His new mom had just finished wiping away her tears and Maddox and Mr. Weldon were shaking hands. "Congratulations to all of you. We couldn't have found a better match if we had tried for a thousand years." He slapped Bobby on the back and although Bobby's eyes were glazed with tears, he could have sworn that he saw moisture in Maddox's eyes too.

When they arrived home, what a great word, he discovered that the room he thought he was helping to decorate for Ricky was actually his. There was a large welcome sign in the kitchen and streamers hanging from the ceiling. He was told many times that evening how welcome he was and how happy they were that he was part of their family. Life was definitely better.

It was the best Christmas he had ever had, and although he wished he could have his mother back, this was the next best thing. He had fun with Ricky while he was home and did many things he had never done before. He played bowls on Friday night, went to the church youth group on Saturday night, and on Sunday they all went to church. He loved singing the hymns. Some of them he recognized from the store music. He loved spending time with Ricky. He was always so serious in the store but he was a lot of fun. On the way home, Ricky asked him if he was planning to go to college in the fall. He thought that it would be great if he went to the same college, because they could share the ride and a room in the college if he was. Bobby told him that he had never thought about college. He said he would like to go some day but he would have to work a while longer to save enough money. Ricky asked his dad at the dinner table if there was any possibility of applying for a scholarship this late in the year. He smiled and told them that he had already been in touch with the college and if his teachers would vouch for him and he satisfied the board during the interviews he was going to be accepted under special circumstances. He was speechless.

# CHAPTER SEVEN

The night before Ricky went back to college he asked Bobbie and his parents if they would come and help the youth choir sing at an old folks home. Some of the regulars had already taken off to college and university and because they have a standing invitation the first Monday of the year to sing for the folks who live there, they did not want to let them down. His mom had promised to do something else but his dad was game, and Bobby said he would go but he was not sure about the singing. Ricky told him that he had a great voice and he would be fine. Most of the songs were the ones his dad played in the store. Evening came and off they went. It felt so good to be part of a real family and he had grown to love and respect this man and his son.

They first went to the church building and met with the pastor, who told them what the program was. They all went in the church bus and invaded the quietness of the old folks home with their cheerful voices and smiles. The old people loved them and asked them to come and visit with the group who stayed in the day room a little longer than the others did. Bobby had never been around older folks before and he loved their enthusiasm. He had watched them as they joined in the singing and was amazed at the reaction to their visitors. They talked eagerly and were interested to know what they were planning for their lives. They ranged from sixty to one hundred years of age. One of the wheelchair bound women asked him what he was planning to do with his life and he found himself telling her about his new family.

She was so happy for him and asked him to come back to visit sometimes. He figured that she was just being polite but he thought that he might like to do that. It would be a way for him to give back some of the joy that he had received that Christmas. He asked her to tell him her name and was surprised to hear that she had his surname. Grandparent sprang into his mind but she told him that she had no family and would welcome a visit anytime. He was disappointed that his first thought was wrong but decided that he would adopt her seeing he did not have a grandma of his own. He felt strangely drawn to a crippled woman who despite being alone in the world had such a good outlook on life. When the day was over and everybody in the church group was getting ready to leave she asked him if he would come back and visit her. He had so enjoyed the day that he readily agreed.

From that day on he became a regular visitor to the home. Sometimes he would bring her flowers or candy. Once he brought her a book and read it to her. While he was reading he would catch her smiling at him. He stopped to ask her if he was doing something wrong. She told him that he was such a sweet boy and was a beautiful reader. Every time he went to see her, her face would light up and her smile of greeting would make his day. She told him often how much his visits meant to her. He would listen to stories she told of her life when she was young. He loved to hear them. His life had been so different. She asked him a few questions about himself but he was reluctant to burden this wonderful old lady with things so ugly. She told him that many years before she had a son about Bobby's age, and a wonderful husband, but that she had lost them both. It was obviously a very painful memory so Bobby did not probe. He just touched her arm and asked if she wanted to go outside. She loved the idea so he wheeled her chair around the grounds and they sat outside for a while.

One day he asked her if she would like to go for an ice cream and she thought that was a great idea. So he wheeled her chair to the ice-cream parlor and they sat and ate together. He could tell that she was glad to be able to leave the walls of her jail, on those occasions and he decided that he would do it as often as he could. One day it started to rain, and he grabbed his jacket and put it on her head and ran as fast as he could safely go back to the home. She was giggling like a girl and he could not help but laugh at the whole incident. She was still laughing when she sent him home so she could take a bath and change her clothes.

One day she told him that her son had left after an argument with them about something. She had forgotten what it was about. He had a very bad temper and yelled at them that he was leaving and never coming back. Her husband had tried to stop him but he had shaken his father off, and knocked him off balance as he slammed the door. Her husband, in an effort to save himself from falling had grabbed a heavy lamp stand. She had risen to help him but he fell anyway and the lamp stand had fallen on her legs and broken them. The fall knocked her husband unconscious and because he was partially on top of her as well as the lamp she couldn't move to help him. It was quite some time before he regained consciousness, but when he did he pulled the lamp away and dragged her to a chair. He was really dizzy and found her too heavy to get to the car so they decided to wait till morning, to go to the doctor. The pain was really bad but she tried not to wake him, because he was so shaken up.

The next morning he was still dizzy and her legs were really swollen so they called an ambulance. She had to have surgery, and they told her that her bones would heal, but there was probably nerve damage, so she might have difficulty walking. Her husband was so supportive and told her that he would help her recover. He came every day to see her and after a week in the hospital she was moved to a nursing home until she could learn to walk. Her husband looked as if he needed more help than her but he insisted that he was fine and tried to help her up a couple of times. He was still so dizzy from the fall that she was concerned. One day he did not come and she had one of her nurses call him at home. There was no answer and she was afraid that he had been in a wreck because of the dizziness. She had the nurse call the police to see if there had been any accidents. They could not help her. She was so anxious that one of her nurses went to her home to see if he was all right. There was no answer so she peeked in the window and saw him on the floor. She sent the paramedics who brought him to the hospital. He had suffered a heart attack, and died two days later. She never saw him again. Bobby was very emotional as he listened to her story. What untold pain this woman had suffered yet she was bright and joyful and loved life. He hugged her and asked if her son had ever returned, and she told him he had not. She was exhausted after telling the story but he was reluctant to leave. Eventually one of the orderlies came by and told him he should really go home.

She slept well that night, surprising herself. She had never told anyone the truth about that day, but she felt that Bobby had a warm heart and she felt comfortable telling him. She made Bobby think about his own grandparents and wondered why they had never come to visit and decided that one day he would find them. He thought about his mother and how isolated his father had made her. He wondered why she had married such a cruel person. Life was strange. Thinking about his mom made him realize how good life had become for him. He thought about Ruthie and wondered if he could have done anymore to help her during the times of violence. Why did people have to hurt one another for no reason? There were many thoughts went through his mind. His decision to have a different kind of life became more and more resolute. He knew that he would treat his wife a lot different, if he ever managed to persuade Anna to marry him.

# CHAPTER EIGHT

School was still a place where Bobby excelled. He was very popular with his teachers. It was refreshing for them to have a serious student. Mr. Weldon had done an extensive search and found a relatively unknown grant, for abandoned children, and he encouraged Bobby to apply. There were a lot of papers to fill out, some by the social workers, and some by his teachers. He told his friend, Mrs. Swanson how surprised and pleased he was at the things everyone had to say about him. She told him it was all true. Finally they were all ready and he mailed them. He found himself saying a prayer as he dropped them in the mailbox. He wondered if God would even hear him or how that all worked. He busied himself at the store to keep from thinking about the result. He suggested some improvements for customer flow in the store and was told to go ahead and if he needed any help he could hire a couple of people for a few days. It meant moving things around in the store. Bobby thought that it would create quite an upheaval and said that he would try and get it all done on Saturday. Mr. Weldon said he would close the store for a couple of days if that would help. Bobby rose early and helped himself to a bagel and some orange juice and was already in the store by seven.

He moved the merchandise to the large cutting table at the back of the store, and then moved the furniture and displays to their new spot. He found the floor needed washing so he set to and was scrubbing that when Mr. Weldon arrived. He was surprised at how much was done. He moved some of the other things according to Bobby's diagram and they were soon finished. He then replaced everything according to the list he had created on the computer at the library. He had used the store laminator to make it sturdier and it was posted at the end of each aisle. They looked at their work with pride and came to the conclusion that a couple of new counter displays would be useful. They were ordered and at one-thirty, they left for the day. They spent the day talking about Bobby's plans and his new foster Dad gave him lots of good advice. Bobby listened carefully. It was so different to have someone genuinely interested in his life. Bobby spoke of his resolve to find Ruthie and Mr. Weldon acknowledged that but told him that he may never find her. He told Bobby that he must find a way to use his experiences to help other people. All in all, it was a very good day and he went to bed content.

School was good that week also. It was their annual Sports Spectacular and there was another school coming to compete with them. The principal had arranged for many sporting events. Tennis was one of them. He had played tennis with Ricky when he was home and had signed up to play at school. He certainly didn't feel up to competing but his teacher said that if everyone played it would be more fun. There were six kids in his class signed up and they were all beginners so he didn't feel so bad. Tuesday, the day before the event, they were allowed to practice during PE that day. The other kids were all laughing but Bobby took everything very seriously, and he was not happy that they were not concentrating. He became upset with them and told them so. One of the boys, who had actually been at Anna's home the fateful day his mother died came over to him and told him to chill and not take things so seriously. His first instinct was to yell at him but he was learning to not react and to consider things before doing anything. He agreed with his friend and the rest of the team came and shook hands with him.

Then they all set to and played tennis. He thought about that later and realized that by being more flexible, he could get more accomplished.

Wednesday dawned and everyone arrived at school early. The

principal had asked him to be one of the greeters for the other school. He checked to see when he played and then went outside to wait for the other school to arrive. He nearly swallowed his teeth when he saw his beloved Anna standing out there too. She was so beautiful. She had her hair tied back off her face and looked radiant. She was so glad to see him again. He loved talking to her. He told her about his mother. Anna was such a good listener. They talked until he heard his name being called, and that it was his turn to play. He did not last long on the court, because his mind was on other things or rather another person, Anna.

When she played he watched her every move. He could not take his eyes of her. She just seemed to float from place to place. His thoughts were bouncing all over his brain. He wondered if her father would allow him to see her now. He wondered how old he had to be to get married. He thought that she looked like one of the heavenly angels, with her blonde hair flying as she moved around the court. She won her set and left the court and came to see if he wanted to get a drink. They spent the rest of the day together, and he walked with her to pick up her brother from his school and then to her home. Just as they arrived her mother drove up and he helped her carry the groceries in from the car. She invited him to stay for a snack but he said he had to get back to work. She told him to come by anytime and he thanked her and left. Anna called after him that she would look for him in the morning. His heart soared. Her parents had not banned him after all.

He talked to his foster mom that night and told her about Anna. She agreed that Anna was a great girl and told him to look after her. She knew Anna's mother and was of the opinion that she would not approve of Anna dating, but thought that it would be all right to invite her over for a meal sometimes. She said that she would talk to Anna's mother and see what she said. The following night Mr. Weldon told him that he could have Wednesday afternoon off.

Bobby was so unassuming; he had no idea what was going on. Anna's mother had told Mrs. Weldon that on Wednesday afternoons there was an after school tennis club that Anna went to. She picked up her son that day so Anna could go. Mr. Weldon figured that if he gave Bobby the day off he would find this out for himself.

He told Anna about it the next day and she told him about the tennis club. He wasted no time in joining and asked Anna if she would go with him to visit his friend at the nursing home afterwards. She said she would but needed to let her mom know. They went and told her mother, then went to visit Mrs. Swanson, and took her out for her ice cream. She was very pleased to meet her and asked her about school and so on. It was a nice visit and Anna was invited to come anytime she wanted.

Anna's dad was home when they arrived, and he stood and talked to Bobby for a few minutes before he left. He invited him for dinner the following Saturday. On that day he discovered that Anna's parents were actually members of the same church as Mr. Weldon. They had not been attending for over a year because her dad had been preaching at another church, about 40 miles away. They were waiting for a new pastor but he was finishing school in another state. The previous pastor had been ill for several months before he died and had asked Anna's dad to help him out. The whole family had been going there, but when the new pastor arrived in June they would be back to their home church. He so enjoyed talking to Anna's dad about the bible that when it came time to go home he realized that he had spent very little time talking to Anna. She had patiently sat there the whole evening just looking at him, very thankful that he was getting along so well with her dad.

Her mom talked to her after Bobby went home, and told her much the same as Mrs. Weldon had told Bobby. She thought it was too soon to be getting involved. They had college to go to and lots of life to live before getting serious and settling down. She thought they should enjoy each other's company as friends, and said that maybe she could invite him for dinner every other week. Anna thought that sounded okay and went to bed happy. The following week the Weldons invited Anna's whole family for dinner and they had a really great time listening to Mr. Weldon's funny stories. A couple of weeks later Anna's parents invited the Weldons for dinner and Bobby of course and that became a monthly pattern. Anna also went with Bobby to the nursing home every Wednesday and one day Mrs. Swanson asked them to sing a hymn to her. She said that she had heard Bobby sing at the beginning of the year but she would love to hear them both. Anna was not too sure about singing, but she looked for a hymn in a book provided by the home and she and Bobby sang. They were in Mrs. Swanson's room, so they felt safe knowing that no one would hear them. When they finished they realized that there were quite a few people congregated around the door, including the director of the nursing home. Everyone told them that their singing was beautiful and the director asked them if they would consider coming back every week to sing for the group. She told them that she was thrilled that Bobby had adopted Mrs. Swanson. She was a different person since he had started visiting her. She wondered if he had any friends who might like to do the same for those in the home who had no one else. Bobby said he would think about it, and on the way home Anna suggested that he talk to the pastor about how to go about it.

He talked to the pastor on Sunday and he thought it was a great idea. The youth group loved to go at the beginning of each year, so he said he would talk to them about making the visit a monthly occurrence instead of an annual one. He invited Bobby to his home that afternoon to discuss the project. He did go to the pastor's home that afternoon and it proved to be one of those earth shattering days. The pastor escorted Bobby to his study and when he entered the room, the number of books astounded him. He told the pastor that it looked like a library. He agreed, but said that his books were a little different to a public library, in that most of the books were theological in nature. Bobby did not know what that meant and asked the pastor. Before they knew it two hours had passed and they had been in deep discussion, without even broaching the nursing home project. The pastor had told Bobby that he could come any afternoon and sit in his study to read any of the books on his shelves. When they finally talked about their project, the pastor asked bobby if he would come to the youth group and explain what he had been doing. He said that it was good for them to hear how other young people were serving Christ. Bobby was taken aback. Serving Christ, he wasn't serving Christ; he didn't even know Christ. He had gathered that he was the Son of God from the pastor's sermons, but that was it. He told the pastor that he knew there was a God because of all that had happened to him but he wasn't sure that he was serving Christ. Their conversation continued with many probing questions from Bobby. These questions included, "What does being saved mean?" and "Why do I need to be saved?" The answers made quite an impression on Bobby. The Holy Spirit was convicting him, and just as Lydia's heart was opened, so was Bobby's. When he was getting ready to go home the pastor prayed with him and asked Bobby if he would like to pray too. He had never, in his life, prayed aloud, but now there didn't seem to be any obstacle, as he poured out his heart before God. When Bobby left the pastor's study that day he was a different person because he now knew Christ, and was committed to serving him.

He couldn't wait to tell Anna, and went to her home. She was so happy she cried because she had experienced God's saving grace while staying at her Grandmother's the previous summer, and had been praying for God to speak to Bobby. He told her he had to go because he wanted to tell the Weldons and everybody about what had happened. She told him to go, that she would see him in school, and off he ran home. His foster parents were very joyful. "No news could be better news" they said. That was a truly happy household that day. That night at church he asked the pastor if he meant it when he told him to come and read. When the pastor reaffirmed the statement, Bobby asked if he could come the following night. The pastor agreed and smiled at his enthusiasm. He had not met many high school seniors who were so excited about books and especially theological books. Bobby became a very regular guest in the pastor's study and they had many long and varied conversations there regarding the things of God.

Bobby did speak to the young people about the residents in the nursing home, and some of them thought that it was a corny idea. There were some who were interested, those whose grandparents lived out of town, and so Bobby outlined what he had done, reading and taking his friend for ice-cream and so on. He was a natural born speaker, and as he outlined the plan he held the attention of every one in that room. The pastor who came in late was amazed at his command of the audience and vowed that he would spend some time encouraging this young man. There were only a few more weeks of school left, so Bobby and the pastor went to tell the nursing home director what their plans were. She was really pleased, and wanted them to start as soon as possible. They decided that as school was almost over, they would start the following Wednesday. They were greeted enthusiastically and before they left, each young person had been adopted by one of the residents, instead of the other way around. Bobby lingered to talk to Mrs. Swanson, who patted his arm and told him he was a good boy. He told her that he had something very important to tell her. She motioned to him to sit down and he started to outline his testimony of how he had been saved and become a Christian a couple of weeks earlier. She was very impressed and asked if it were possible for her to go to church with him. He was thrilled and said that he would pick her up bright and early each Sunday morning and they would go to church together. He also told her that he had tried to see his sister before school ended but was not able to find her and felt that he had lost contact with her because he would not be going back to school.

She was sad because she knew how much Bobby wanted to have his family all united again.

It was with great pride that he wheeled his friend into church on Sunday morning. He sat with her and she sang along with the hymns. He was excited about that and in fact encouraged the other young people to ask if their adopted friends would like to come to church. There were quite a few who did start coming regularly and it thrilled Bobby that he had had a little part to play in that. Mrs. Swanson started asking a lot of questions when he visited and one day she announced to him that she had been converted to Christ. He was beside himself. Nothing could have thrilled him more. What a wonderful God to not only save him but his dear friend too. He hugged her so tightly that day that she had to tell him she needed to breathe, whereupon they both dissolved in to laughter. Anna had not been able to go that day and he had to go and give her the good news. He wanted to share everything good with Anna.

A few weeks later, Mr. Weldon received a call from the nursing home. They needed Bobby to come over that afternoon. It was not Wednesday, so he asked if he could be late to work. He was worried that there was something wrong and he found it difficult to concentrate that day in school. He saw Anna and asked her to pray about it. After school he raced over to the home, and found his fears unfounded. Mrs. Swanson was sitting in her room looking like the cat that had swallowed the canary. He asked her what was wrong and she said that he would have to be patient for a few more minutes. The director came and poked her head in the door and said that her lawyer would be about fifteen minutes. Mrs. Swanson then told Bobby that her son had abandoned her more that twenty years before and that her husband was dead and she had no one in the world but him. Bobby was inclined to fear that she was ill or something but she just seemed so excited that he was quite bewildered. His friend went on to say that she owned some land in Nebraska. It had been in her family for years and she had no siblings, so it had come to her. A few years ago oil had been discovered there and the government had offered to buy the land. She had dithered about selling it but because she knew that she would never see the land and had no one to leave it to she had sold it. Yesterday she had had a visit from a lawyer who informed her that she was a very wealthy woman. She told Bobby that she had no need for money and wanted him to have it. She believed that God had a purpose for it and she was sure that He would reveal that purpose to Bobby when the time was right.

Bobby told her that he could absolutely not take the money and suggested that one day her son might come back. She became quite upset with Bobby and started crying. He told her that he did not want to upset her but that much as he loved her he was not her family and he didn't think it would be legal. She said that she would legally adopt him if that were what it would take but that it was all sealed and settled and that the lawyer was on his way to have Bobby sign the papers and become her heir.

It was not long before he indeed arrived, and in a very businesslike way he explained again what his friend had just told him. He needed Bobby's signature and then it would be a little while before the money would become available. It would not all be available at once, because her lawyer had worked out the best deal as far as taxes etc. Bobby sat there stunned. He questioned in his heart what plan God had for him and what all this meant. They all shook hands and the lawyer started to leave when Mrs. Swanson asked the lawyer about how much the total was. His answer stunned both of them. He said that there would be quite a lot of fees but he thought that in the end when all the taxes were paid and if they didn't take it all at once there would be approximately three million dollars. Bobby sat down again. He could not even conceive of that amount of money. He looked at the papers the lawyer had left, including names of financial advisers who were Christians and hopefully reputable. He looked at the statements in front of him and was glad they had been explained to him because he barely understood the legalese. After he had time to absorb everything he asked his friend why she would do such a thing. She told him that he was a dear boy and she loved him. She knew that one day God would use him to do great things and she wanted to help. She said that she trusted him to do the right thing with the money. She told him to go home and talk to his foster parents and let them help him decide what he should do with the money, and to find out what was necessary for him to be legally adopted by her.

He left in a daze, went by the store and found it closed, went home and discovered that it was already 7 PM. He told The Weldons everything that had transpired and they were also stunned. He told them about the adoption and asked if that was possible. They knew someone who actually arranged adoptions so they would know what to do. He slept little, and could think of nothing else that next day. Days went by in a blur, but with the help of friends who knew friends the adoption was arranged and he wheeled a very excited old friend to the lawyer's office. She was given the papers to sign. She stared at them for quite a while and the lawyer asked her if she was having second thoughts. She didn't speak and Bobby was a little embarrassed. She looked at Bobby and for once he could not read her thoughts. He told her that it was okay, that she could change her mind. She still did not speak. The lawyer was getting a little impatient, and Bobby asked her if she wanted to go back home. She shook her head from side to side. Bobby looked at the lawyer who made a questioning motion with his hands. Bobby said that he would leave for a few minutes and let her talk to the lawyer, but she finally found her voice and said, "Your father was my son". Now it was the turn of the lawyer and Bobby to be silent. "You are my grandson, I am your grandmother", she said weeping unashamedly. "Oh Bobby, You dear boy, all this time and I never even asked your parents names." Bobby had difficulty absorbing the news. The lawyer recovered first. "You mean that you didn't know that this was your grandson?" "No! No! I had no idea. This says that his father signed relinquishment papers, so he is still alive. Does he live around here? Where is he?" "I don't know the answer to any of your questions. I found out that information from the social worker who worked their case. They found him in the criminal justice system. At that time he was in another state and had managed to get him to sign relinquishment papers for all three of the children at the same time. He could tell her no more than that. He had not needed to look for him, because he had all that he needed to go ahead with the adoption. He was a little bewildered that neither of them knew that they were related. She suddenly started laughing and somehow that broke the spell of silence Bobby had dissolved into. He went to her and hugged her saying "Grandma I am so happy. How could I not have known?" She said, "So Ruthie and Lillian are my grandchildren too."

They went ahead and signed the papers, and then they left to go back to the nursing home, two very happy people. Bobby asked her if she wanted to buy a home for them and they could live together and he would help her. She told him that she was very content and would stay where she was for the present. He was amazed that she had all this money and was content to stay in this home. She told him that ever since she had met him she had felt like the richest woman in the world, and that money was not needed to make her feel that way.

He could not wait to tell Anna, so he went by her home and her family was so pleased. Anna and her mom both cried a little, because Bobby was so choked up about finding his Grandmother. "God has already answered one of my prayers, do I dare hope that he will help me find Ruthie. If relinquishment papers were signed, she could already be adopted and changed her name and, and." Anna's father put his arm around Bobby's shoulders and said, "Come on Bobby, This is not a time to be worrying about such things. God can move mountains and make the world stop moving so I think that He probably knows where Ruthie is." Bobby knew that he was right and soon left to tell his foster parents. They were even more excited than Bobby if that was possible. "She can come and stay with us if you like; we can't have your Grandma living in a nursing home." They talked it over and decided that it would be difficult with the stairs and everything. He said he would discuss it with her next day. He was told that he didn't need to come into work the rest of the week so he could get things sorted out. He went to bed for another night of fitful sleep as he tried to let the news sink in. He had so many questions, like why had God waited until he had lost touch with Lillian before letting him know about his Grandmother, and would this revelation make a difference to his being able to bring Ruthie back home. He decided that he would return to Holman House and find out as soon as he could. Next morning he told the folks at breakfast what he had planned to do. They agreed that he should go, that his news changed everything. However they thought that he needed to check with his grandmother before making any plans. They reminded him that he had mail from the previous day. He opened the letter and read that he had been accepted into the same college as Ricky. He started off being excited and then he asked them if he could still go to college because he had new responsibilities, like taking care of his grandmother. Also he was not abandoned anymore, so he didn't deserve the scholarship, now what was he to do. His foster parents told him to calm down, and take one step at a time. Mr. Weldon offered to make the calls for him if he wanted to go and talk things over with his grandmother.

She told him that he must go to college and that if he didn't have the scholarship then that is what he must use the money for. She did tell him to go and find out what he could about Ruthie, and to ask some of the kids from school if they knew where Lillian was. If he knew where she lived he could try again and at least give her the option of coming to live with them. She really wanted to stay at the nursing home until all was settled, and was glad to wait until Bobby finished college. He went straight over to Holman House and enquired again about Ruthie's situation. Apparently her foster parents had changed their minds and she was brought back to Holman House, but refused to get out of the car. She had become hysterical so they had gotten in touch with another county, who agreed to help them out and take her to a different Rescue Home. Since then her case had been taken over by that county and all her files had been sent. They were unable to disclose any further information to Bobby. He tried to tell them that he had found his grandmother and that she could now come home to live with them. They asked him where his grandmother lived and he told them that she lived in a nursing home. They said a child couldn't live in a nursing home. He tried to explain that they were going to buy a home. They thought his story was a bit hard to believe and told him that he was wasting their time and his own and to let it drop. He asked if he could speak with Maddox, and they told him that he was gone for a few days but that they would let him know that he had come by.

He went back to the store and found out that because of the money he had inherited, the board would have to rethink the situation. They would be meeting the following week. Bobby said that he would just as soon work as be home thinking all these confusing thoughts. At lunchtime Mr. Weldon asked him if he still wanted to continue working there. Bobby was suddenly afraid that his good fortune was going to bereave him of one of the stabilizing things in his life. He looked at Mr. Weldon with such panic in his eyes that His boss told him that he only asked, because now he was a wealthy young man and didn't need to work. Bobby became quite tearful and told Mr. Weldon that he did need to work, that this was where he wanted to work always, that in his dreams of growing up this was where he saw himself and to please not turn him out. They both had a very emotional lunch break and when it was over they embraced and Mr. Weldon told Bobby that he was the best thing that had ever happened to him, besides his own family.

Bobby went back to see his grandmother next day and asked if he should use the money to get her a better place to live. He wanted to buy a home for them but if he were going to college he would not be there to look after her. She told him that she wasn't giving him all the money and that she had already taken care of things in the nursing home. She was moving to a bigger room, and was giving a tenth of the money to the church. He just needed to settle down and do what he always did, and not worry about what to do with the money. She advised him to keep it quiet which others had advised him to do. She told him that God would let him know what to do. He asked her if she wanted to go out to celebrate and she agreed. She felt as if she were young again, and was happier to see Bobby's excitement than she was to get the money. He invited the Weldons, Anna and her parents, and called the pastor to see if he could borrow the church van. It had a lift for a wheelchair, so his grandmother could travel to the restaurant. On the following Saturday, Mr. Weldon drove to Anna's home and picked up the family, then on to the nursing home and found Bobby and his Grandmother. She was all dressed up in a fine new dress, which Bobby had bought for the occasion. She was smiling so widely. This was what she had always longed for ...to be part of a family. The two families could hardly believe that this was the same woman they had met at Christmas. She was like a new woman.

Mrs. Weldon sat beside Bobby's grandmother and they talked non-stop. Before they took Mrs. Swanson home she had been invited to come to the monthly gatherings at the Weldon's home.

# CHAPTER NINE

The pastor had given Bobby charge over the youth group and he had gotten permission to have Anna help him. Her parents were thrilled. She had always been so shy and never wanted to take part in anything, which meant she had to be up in front of people. She gladly consented to help Bobby, however and her parents remarked that they had noticed that Bobby had a way of drawing her out and letting her shine. They approved wholeheartedly. They started the next week and all went well. The young people already liked Bobby and they all took part without much persuasion, except for one boy in the group. He would not join in; in fact, he acted as if he did not want to be there. He just kept looking at the door. Bobby tried to talk to him after wards, but he was in a big hurry to go even though the others were all going for ice cream. Bobby had a flashback to his own life a couple of years before when he opted out of everything, even though he would really have loved to stay. He went to visit Simon at home, and found that the mother was ill, but they had no insurance and no money, and the father had lost his job, Bobby asked why, Terry, the dad had been laid off and he said that his car had broken down and needed an expensive repair job. He had tried to work on it himself but could not get it fixed and he had been laid off because of absenteeism. He had tried to find work nearer home but so far had not found anything. They were running out of money for food because it had been two weeks and now his wife was sick and he did not know what to do. He was angry with himself because he was not being a good provider and his anger was manifesting itself in his impatience with his wife and children. He seemed relieved to be able to talk to someone about it all. Bobby knew that God had brought him there, and had already decided that he could help these folks. Bobby asked the dad if he could come with him for a coffee. The father was puzzled but agreed. It was better than sitting there feeling sorry for him. Bobby asked him if his car was repaired would he be able to get his job back. He said that he would call and find out. Then he told him to call and have his car towed to the repair shop near the hardware store. Bobby waited until the tow truck came and paid the driver. Then he went to the bank and drew out some money, took it back to the father and told him to let him know whether or not he was able to get his job back. The father asked Bobby if he knew anyone who would take his wife to the Urgent Care Clinic, and Bobby called Mr. Weldon.

He came right over and between them they managed to get the sick woman into the car. Bobby stayed to take care of the kids. Simon was already looking a little happier, and when his parents came home and said that his mom had bronchitis and would be all right he burst out crying, and told her that he thought she was going to die like their grandparents. While the parents were gone he had discovered that there was very little food in the house, so after they got home he went to the 24-hour grocery and bought food for them, including ice cream. He told Steve that he had brought it because he had missed it earlier. Terry and his wife were overwhelmed at Bobby's generosity but when they told him, he said that the gifts were not from him but from God. The following Sunday the whole family were at church, Mom was feeling much better, Dad was starting work next day, his car was fixed and they told Bobby that they would pay him as soon as they could. Bobby grinned and told them that God did not expect to be paid back and to just thank Him. He used the opportunity to say that because of what God had done for him he was able to help out other people. He reminded them that God had sent His son to die for the sins of His people because He loved them. They had tears in their eyes as they left, and Bobby thought that perhaps he would go and visit them again soon.

The next youth meeting found Simon a changed person; he joined in the activities and singing and asked Bobby if there was anything he could do for him. After the meeting, everyone stayed around talking. They all loved to talk to Bobby and tell him of their dreams for the future. He was only a couple of years older but they liked the way he showed them respect, and they in turn respected him. Bobby used every opportunity to tell them how much better life was when it was lived for the Lord. He told them that his life was so much happier and stable since God was directing things. They had many questions and listened intently as he patiently answered them.

The church members noticed that they were much better behaved in recent weeks and the pastor told them about Bobby. He loved passing on to them the things he learned in the pastor's study each week. He still continued to spend several hours a week reading and asking his own questions. The pastor was very impressed with this young man as he was a quick learner and had such a special gift with people. He told the young people that they needed to call him Mr. Swanson, but Bobby disagreed and told them that made him feel too old, But he agreed with the pastor and told them that they could call him Mr. Bob. They liked that idea and decided that Mr. Bob would be his new title.

Bobby felt very blessed with his life as he made preparations for college. He would miss everyone so much. He would not see the young people, his Grandmother, his dear friends, the Weldon's, the love of his life, Anna, and the pastor who had become his mentor and teacher of all things spiritual, for quite a while. His life was full of good things and good people. His God was a faithful God.

# CHAPTER TEN
## (EIGHT YEARS LATER)

Junior High had brought a myriad of change for the three friends, Julie, Rachel and Marie. They had decided during summer break that they would go and choose their electives together so that they would all be able to stay in the same class. They had met in grade school and were like sisters rather than friends. At the end of sixth grade, Carla's family moved to another state and they lost touch. The others talked about her all the time, and vowed that one day they would find her again. In seventh grade, they were split up again. Julie's dad was the assistant pastor in Beracha Baptist church and that year their pastor, Dr Fletcher died. He was such a kind man and they all knew him because he was often a visitor at Julie's home. He had a fatal heart attack, and the anguish Julie felt made her feel as if she had heart pain too. Marie's mother was a nurse, and she encouraged Julie by telling her that anxiety causes pain and that she was not going to die. They consoled Julie and each other and gradually the hurt lessened. Later however the anxiety returned when Julie's dad was called as the pastor to the church and they had to move to the home on the church property. She had to move to another school. It seemed like the end of the world to them. She was able to stay until the end of the semester but they all felt as if their hearts would break. That summer they spent a lot of time together, and went to summer camp with Julie. They had a lot of fun but they also had many very serious talks about eternity. Julie was a Christian, and had no misgivings about talking to her friends about salvation and the Lord Jesus Christ. It was a mystery, especially for Marie whose parents did not go to church. She often thought about what would happen if she were to die, and where she would spend eternity. They were reaching the stage in life when children realize that change is all there is.

In eighth grade, Marie's father who was in the Reserve was mobilized and sent to Iraq. Her mom went back to her work at the hospital because his wages were not going to cover their bills. Marie was almost as upset about that as she was about her father. Her dad was a serious person, not much for playing with them outside like Julie and Rachel's fathers did, but never the less, she was going to miss the long talks with him, sitting on the porch. She was also going to miss her Mom. She had enjoyed the fact that her mom was always home, and would play card games with her in the evening after schoolwork was done. It annoyed her that things had to change.

When school was out Marie would ride her bike to Rachel's and then her mom would pick her up when she finished work at eight. They spent their time doing homework or just hanging out, or swimming. Sometimes they would play basketball and Rachel's older brother would show off his skills and teach them a few moves. Marie liked him but he was a senior and had a girlfriend and she did not much care for Marie so when she was there Rachel and Marie would walk. Despite the challenges, time had brought their way eighth grade graduation day dawned and their excitement grew to a climax. They were going to high school and would all be together again. If only Carla could be there too.

Julie's graduation was the same night, but her dad brought her over so they could all be together for the night. They were all spending the night in Rachel's and they stayed up until two o'clock in the morning, talking about high school, and how fun it would be. Next day three sleepy girls asked Rachel's dad if he would help them find Carla, so they could write to her. A couple of weeks later, they got together again at Julie's and Rachel said that she had a surprise for them. They could not wait to hear what it was. She said that they would have to wait until after supper.

They were relentless asking her to tell them and when she did, they were whooping and hollering like little kids because her dad had found Carla's address. They all wrote pages and mailed the letter. They were so impatient waiting for a reply that their parents were getting a little tired of them... They promised that they would not ask anymore, but their patience was not tried any further because they received a letter from Carla. She wrote pages and pages. She missed them so and asked if she could come and stay for a while. Her parents had told her it would be okay.

Rachel's mom talked to Carla's mom and it was all arranged. Rachel's mom also said that all four of them could stay if it was all right with their parents. They couldn't wait but when the time came the vacation went much too fast and was soon over. Carla thought she would like her new school; she had been to visit while her sister was going there. Now her sister was going to college and she was going to have to listen to her griping and complaining about that... She wished she could be back with her friends to stay. Life was not like that, she decided. She spent a long time one night talking to Julie about spiritual things. She told Julie that God had shown her how sinful she was and how He had sent His son, the Lord Jesus Christ into the world to die for sinners like her. Julie and she had prayed together and rejoiced that they had something very important in their lives to share.

Carla's sister had caused her parent's some grief because she did not like their rules. She had the idea that when she went to college she would be free of them. Now they had followed her and she was mad. Carla's dad was given two choices and this felt like the best one. They felt that their older daughter needed more guidance. They were less concerned about Carla; she was so sweet and submitted willingly to their rules. It was always a treat when she was at home, and that is why they felt very comfortable with allowing her to go on this trip.

Rachel's mom looked out the window. The girls were all playing together and laughing so much. She was so glad that Carla had been able to come. They had missed her so much. She wondered what they would all be doing in 10 years. How she would like to protect them from the sad side of life, but she knew she could not. She would just enjoy these years when they were all more or less carefree. They would have to experience the good and the bad in life, but right now it was fun time. She filled a pitcher of lemonade and carried it out to the deck. She asked them if they wanted to go to a movie later, but they were having too much fun, and decided to just hang out at home.

Later that evening, Marie had a call from her mother. She had been promoted to charge nurse. They decided to throw her a party. Next day they got to work right away planning the event. Marie called her mom's friends and invited them to come on her mom's next evening off. Rachel's mom volunteered to help them with the refreshments. Marie ordered a cake. She was so excited that she had friends who would help her do this for her mom. They all helped with the decorations and the invitations. They went to Marie's home the day of the party and decorated the front porch, and were all hiding when her mom came home. She was so surprised when her friends all came. Marie's dad called and heard about the promotion. He also said that he thought that he might be home by Marie's birthday. They were so happy with tears all around. They had permission to stay at Marie's that night so they could clean up the next day. Marie spent a long time talking to Carla out on the porch. It sounded very serious, so everyone left them alone though they were dying to know what it was all about.

They cleaned up next day and the day after Carla had to go home. They were so sad, and made up their minds that they would go to the same college. And they would get together every summer. They hugged and cried and hugged again. When the boarding call came they hooked their fingers together and made a vow to stay in touch, and Carla was gone.

Julie went home too because she was traveling with her mother to help their grandparents pack. They were moving closer to their family. Julie told her friends that they would have to go back in a couple of weeks to clean up the house and wondered if they wanted to go and help. She was hoping but was really surprised when they all agreed.

They all traveled in the mini-van, and although they had to work really hard they enjoyed being together, and got the job done quickly. The grandparents were sent by plane and that left room in the van for the rest of the stuff the movers had left behind. On the way home Julie's mom drove to a lake resort, and spent the night. They stayed there the next day and begged to stay another night. They left at noon the following day and when they got home they found the grandparents all settled in. Julie's uncle, her dad's younger brother, had just received orders for him to go to Iraq. He had been staying with them, waiting for his orders. Julie's dad announced the news on Sunday morning. Everyone was sad to see him go. Everyone was encouraged to pray for him while he was gone.

Julie's grandparents found a home really close to them and she visited them every week. Somehow Marie and Rachel managed to come every week as well and sometimes they all visited the grandparents together. Grandma taught them to knit and do cross-stitch. Also they did some baking and cooking, and really loved spending time with them. However the summer was soon over and school was soon to start again.

Their junior year started uneventfully except that Carla called and told Rachel to tell Marie to call her next evening. Rachel wondered what the mystery was but figured that she would hear soon enough. Meantime at Julie's church they had a new youth pastor. Julie thought he was great. He was a good teacher and his wife was really sweet. He was planning a special youth program during school break and wanted them all to invite their friends from school. Julie was excited and asked Marie and Rachel. They both said that they would go. Roll on Thanksgiving. Because they both agreed to go she invited them to the

Friday evening Young People's meeting. They went the following week and Mr. Swanson was very interesting, and his wife was really sweet. He did a skit in which he was helping some homeless people, and one of them called him Brother Bob. The name stuck and from then on everyone in the church called him Brother Bob. At the meeting he divided the kids into groups of six and gave them questions. They had to write their answers down and then come back together and tell the group. It was interesting to hear the different viewpoints. Brother Bob validated each group's thoughts and very skillfully showed that each person, although different had his or her own worth. It was the same with the skit. He wanted the young people to know that each one of them was important in the eyes of the Lord.

When Marie got home she talked non-stop about the meeting. Her mother was very interested in all Marie had to say. She told Marie that her dad had called again and had asked if they could go to church when he came home. She told Marie that if she liked they could go to that church. Marie was very happy. The following Sunday they went to church together. Her dad called again on Sunday afternoon and he talked and talked about what God had done for him. He became quite emotional so didn't explain it all, just asked again if they could go to church when he got home. Marie's mom told him that they had already gone that morning. He was surprised but said nothing.

The following week Rachel came with her parents and her brother. He had broken up with his girlfriend and came to find out about the youth pastor he had heard about. He talked to Brother Bob for quite a while after church.

# CHAPTER ELEVEN

Marie and her mother had been going to church for about one month when they got a very exciting letter from her dad. They read together that he was really on his way home. They were giddy with excitement. Her mom knew that things were going to be different in their home from now on. Her husband was a different person. The conflict with which he was involved had changed him, she thought for the better. He had never been a very talkative person, but now he his letters was verbose. She felt a thrill, like she was meeting him for the first time. He told them that he wasn't sure what day he would be home but that it would be soon.

In church that Sunday, the pastor also had good news. His younger brother, who was also on active duty had been in touch with them and was expected home very soon. When the pastor spoke of his brother he became very emotional and it was obvious to all that he had been very concerned about him. Everyone who knew the family was so happy to hear the news. Someone in the congregation told the pastor about Marie's dad coming home and he made a point of telling her mother how happy he was for them, and that he would like to come one day and visit with them when her husband was home and settled in.

Meantime Marie had asked her friends if they would help her make a welcome home poster for her dad, and they spent part of every day that week doing so. They made one for Julie's uncle as well so they stayed pretty busy. Senior year was in full swing; the girls had finagled their seat assignments so that in every class except one they sat together. In Art class, however the teacher wanted them to sit in alphabetical order, so they were scattered throughout the room. They couldn't wait till the end of the class to get together again. After the first class Rachel was really upset. She had been assigned to sit beside a very rude, loud-mouthed girl called Nomed, who wore her black hair covering most of her face. She looked positively scary, because when her face did show she had black eye shadow and black lipstick. Her Goth style of dressing made her stand out in the class, but it was the obscenities she spouted every time she opened her mouth, which made Rachel, upset. She told her friends that this girl's attitude was as black as the clothes she wore. "She says them quietly enough that the teacher does not hear, just me. I don't think I can bear to sit with her the whole year. I may have to give up Art." She went to the office to try and change her elective but found that she was going to have to switch all of her other classes and take advanced math as her elective so she resigned herself to the fact that she was going to have a miserable year in Art class.

In youth group, Brother Bob had told them if they had a problem that they could not solve they should talk to a grownup about it. She thought about talking to her parents but knew they could do nothing about her predicament. She found that Nomed would take up most of the space at the table leaving very little room for Rachel. Also she would knock Rachel's supplies to the floor and laugh at her frustration. She became very resentful and her frustration spilled over even when she was with her friends. They told her to chill out and that made her cross. She felt that she was misunderstood and that her life was unfair. At youth group she was quiet. Then when Brother Bob asked his wife to sing with him, Rachel was so envious of her. She thought Anna had such a perfect life, perfect baby, perfect husband and she always looked so happy. They were always helping other people and everyone loved them. She wondered why her life could not be like that. Instead she has to sit beside this odious creature who liked nothing and nobody. Her attitude grew worse as the days passed. She was really upsetting Marie and Julie and soon her parents were worried about her as well.

Her mother asked her if all was well with her friends and she mumbled something about them not knowing what she had to put up with. She answered her mother's further questions by saying that she didn't want to talk about it. Her father talked to her as well and found the same blank wall. He thought that they should talk to Marie and Julie and try to find out what was eating at her.

That week at youth group Brother Bob chose to talk about the troubles people have to face in life. He told them that God's children would never experience anything, which was not for their good. Rachel sat and muttered to herself that he had no idea what he was talking about. She was feeling very sorry for herself and started thinking along the lines that perhaps she was not one of God's children, because what she had to bear was certainly not for her good. She decided that she was not going to come to youth group any more. She felt that they didn't know what they were talking about. She refused to go to church on Sunday and her parents were surprised but didn't argue with her. They did however talk to the pastor and to Brother Bob to see if they had any ideas.

The pastor's brother had arrived and was at church that Sunday. The Pastor made him stand up and everybody smiled and nodded to him. Then they all started to clap their hands. He was embarrassed, and told them that he was no hero, that they should be thanking the guy that saved his life. This guy is the real hero and was badly injured by the explosion, which should have killed him and his captain. He was too emotional to give any more details, but it was enough information for the pastor to decide that a time of prayer for Joe, the young man in question, was necessary. When Rachel's parents arrived home they were talking about Peter (the pastor's brother) and what he had said. They also told Rachel that Peter was going to be speaking at youth group that week. Rachel felt a twinge of shame when she thought of what Peter had experienced. She decided to go back to youth group just to hear his story.

Some of the young people had put the banners up welcoming Peter home. Peter was delighted and when Brother Bob asked him to come and talk about how God had protected him while in Iraq, they all clapped again. Peter stood up and started to tell them about his stay in this war torn country. Some of the young men were thinking about joining one of the branches of the military so he had their full attention. A very short time after he had started speaking there was a definite hush came over all those gathered there.

Peter recounted arriving in Iraq and finding only horror. He felt sorry for the people there whose lives were engulfed in war. He told them of the suicide bombers and their lack of emotion, as they drove their vehicles into the path of American soldiers who were only there to help them. They had no thought for the lives of the civilians who happened to be walking by or of their own lives. He told them about little children who were killed or injured as a result of these attacks. He told them that the only thing, which kept him strong during all this mayhem, was the knowledge, that God was with him. He thanked them for praying for him when he was gone, and said that he had prayed more often there than ever before. He said that he had stayed in an attitude of prayer the whole time he was gone, because he really didn't know if he would live for the next five minutes. He said that one soldier called Joe came to him one day and told him that he was spooking him because he was always talking to himself. He told the guy that he was not talking to himself but that he was talking to God. This soldier was the slowest person he had ever met; he had to think about everything before he did it. He was always the last person up in the morning, the last person ready. He irritated everyone. They gave him the nickname Slow Joe. Peter said that Slow Joe was a little taken aback when he told him about God. He said he didn't believe there was a god otherwise they wouldn't be there dodging bullets and bombs. Peter had told him that God wasn't responsible for the atrocities they witnessed daily, that men who denied God were the cause. He told Joe that God had made the world and everything in it was perfect until men had fouled it up. God was not the instrument of evil but men had corrupted God's handiwork. He had told Joe that God even before he made the world and all the people in it had decided to send His Son into the world as a man so that He would die to pay for the sins which humankind had committed.

Joe's answer was that Peter had to be kidding. Peter said that it was the truth, that Jesus, God's Son died that we might be forgiven. Joe then said that he wanted to know more about this God because he had a lot which he needed forgiveness for. Peter said that his platoon leader came at that point to give then their orders. Their captain gave them their usual warning about being vigilant and staying safe. Look out for the other guy but protect yourself first. You can't help anyone if you are dead. His warning reminded them of the stark reality of their situation. He proceeded to read their names from the ledger, sending them out in groups of three. There had been some activity near the perimeter of their camp and they needed to secure the camp. Peter told them that his name was not called to the end and he was a little nervous when he realized that he and Joe were the only ones left. Joe sure would not have been his choice as a partner. Before he had time to form any thoughts on the subject the captain himself told them that he was making up their threesome? He remembered thinking about how he was telling Joe about God and now was wishing that he could be anywhere Joe wasn't. He quickly chided himself for his lack of faith not in Joe but in his God, and prayed for their safety as they moved in the dark. Peter was the rear lookout and Joe the forward. He had his weapon poised and ready for any sudden moves on the part of the enemy.

The next thing he knew he was flying through the air with such force, he couldn't imagine what had hit him in the back. He fell heavily to the ground and lay there for a second or two catching his breath and feeling a tremendous weight on top of him. Suddenly the thing on top of him moved and he turned as fast as his battle gear would allow him. It was his captain. Both of them said in one voice "What was that?" Neither of them heard the other. They were deaf. They both stood up and Peter said he staggered a little and the captain steadied him while they looked around to see what had hit them. He discovered a nasty bump on his head which was making him dizzy. He had hit the ground rather hard.

They were both thinking that something rather large had hit them. They had heard no engine, and were thinking maybe an animal had charged them. There was nothing to be seen... No vehicle; no animal; nothing. What they did see, in the darkness 3 or 4 yards away, in the spot where they had been standing, was Joe lying very still with his face on the ground. They were on the camp side of the ridge, so they quickly looked to see if they were safe and crawled over to Joe. His back was bare and bloody, and he was unresponsive. The captain sent Peter for the medics by using sign language and he ran faster than he had ever run before. Taking the medics back to the spot, they moved the unconscious soldier back to the tent. They cut off the rest of his uniform and poured sterile saline on the wound and then covered his back with saline soaked gauze. The captain indicated to the medics that Peter needed to lay down. Then he turned and left. Pretty soon a helicopter arrived minus lights and cautiously set down near the tents. Before getting to the helicopter Joe awoke and started screaming in pain. He had to be subdued with pain medication before they could get him in the aircraft. He was almost asleep again but as he was being moved in he murmured "Are Cap and Pete ok? I tried to push them away. I shoved them as hard as I could. Then he was asleep again. The chaplain was nearest to him at that time and told the captain what Joe had said. The captain came over to where I was laying and wrote this on a piece of paper We realized then that Joe had seen what was coming and had pushed us with superhuman strength out of harms way. We were both pretty shaken up by the whole thing and the cap wrote that he couldn't understand how one person could move two grown men so far. Peter told how he bowed his head and thanked God for His protection, and asked for healing for Joe. When He opened his eyes the captain was praying too. They wrote notes to each other and Peter told about his misgivings at being assigned with Joe, because he didn't feel safe with him and now he felt so bad because Joe had saved his life and was so badly injured. They agreed to visit Joe as soon as they could to thank him for his bravery.

Peter stated that when he went to bed that night, sleep did not come easy. He had thought about his family back home. He knew that they were praying for him and He thanked God for that and for the protection God had afforded him. He thought over and over about the incident and how near death he had come. He had eventually slept and woke next day to the touch of his captain. He still could not hear, so they wrote to one another. I tried to get up and get dressed but my body was fairly well covered with bruises and Captain helped me to get dressed. He wanted to know more about this God of mine who could give such superhuman power to someone like Slow Joe to enable him to move at the speed of light. Peter was able to tell the captain that not only did He send Joe to save our lives that day but that He had sent His Son to die for us, so that we could live for eternity. The captain and he had scribbled notes for some time. And then in the middle of a war had knelt and talked to God himself. God opened the heart of that captain and he arose from his knees, a changed man. His ambition was now to tell his family about his wonderful Lord. He started a letter to his wife at once. It had taken another week before he and his captain were able to be outside again. Their hearing gradually returned but in the interval many notes were written about God and His salvation.

Six months later, they received orders to move to a different area because the guerillas had gone to a more desolate place. A week later, they received the glad news that they were going home. The captain had been able to locate Joe in a Belgium hospital, and was to move stateside in about ten days. He was doing ok but had a long recovery ahead of him. He had asked Peter if he wanted to meet up with him and go to see Joe. Peter said that he would like to thank the man who had saved his life.

The captain had written a report of Joe's actions and had been summoned to Washington to make his statement to a panel of military personnel. Peter went with him to Washington, where he would catch a plane to Texas, where he would be given his new orders. They were able to travel together to the airport and the captain asked him for his address so he could keep in touch. He said that the world is so small because he found out that his captain lives right here in our town. He has promised to come to church as soon as he gets here. I will be going with him to see Joe and asked everyone to pray for this young man who had saved his life.

When he sat down there was silence. No one moved or spoke for a few minutes. Even Brother Bob was at a loss for words. What an experience. When He finally stood up, he closed the meeting in prayer. He felt that there were no other words needed. The young people began to speak in hushed tones. Marie was particularly moved. She had no idea that her dad could be in that kind of danger, and was glad that he was coming home. She would tell him about Peter and his captain and Joe. She hoped that her dad had friends like that in his company. She would tell him that he should come to church and meet this other captain. Oh, she could not wait to see him. She was glad to see Rachel there and went over to talk to her. Rachel said that she was sorry for being so obnoxious and for making such a commotion over nothing. She had been thinking that perhaps she would ask Nomed to come to youth group and wondered if she and Julie would go with her when she was asking her. Marie said that she would be glad to, and then went home with Rachel because her Mom was working late. The girls all talked together about Peter's story. They wondered if God really did care about what they did in their individual lives. Brother Bob certainly thought so and Julie's dad and uncle thought so. But what about them? Did they matter to God? Could they have a close relationship with him? They pondered these questions and were rather subdued when Marie's mother arrived. Marie told her mom about Peter's story and then they sat up half the night talking about God. They decided that they would talk to the pastor about their questions and particularly about salvation.

# CHAPTER TWELVE

Next day at class Rachel sighed as she made her way to sit beside Nomed. She had promised her friends that she would have a better attitude. Nomed did not co-operate however and really taxed her resolve to the limits. They were supposed to be making a hand out of clay. The fingers were proving to be difficult and she looked at Nomed to see what she was doing. She still had her ball of clay. Rachel went to the teacher for help and when the teacher came near their table Nomed swore and started to work on her clay. The teacher showed Rachel how to bend the fingers a little and then turned to Nomed and asked what she was doing. Named said that she was working on a hand. At the end of the class, they placed their hands on the side counter and there in the middle was Nomed's hand rolled into a tight fist. It looked menacing among all the outstretched hands. Rachel thought again, about how weird she was but was determined to ask her. Her heart would beat a little faster when she thought about it. She met her friends after class and decided that now was as good a time as ever to do the asking so they stood at the door and waited for her. When she appeared at the door, they moved towards her. She stopped to fix her shoe and when she stood upright, they were all standing in front of her. Nomed was taken aback, she usually kept everyone a little afraid of her so they would not enter her space and here were these three just marching into it. She was amazed at how hard it was to get a reaction from Rachel. She had tried her best to get her upset since the start of the year and Rachel never once had answered her. She glowered at them but they were determined not to be afraid, even though their hearts were thumping. We would like to invite you to youth group next week. Nomed was astounded, could not believe her ears. She had thought they were going to attack her for being so mean and she was ready for that but this… She had no quick answer ready. She swore and tried to brush past them. They called after her." Its on Wednesday at 7pm, we could meet you and …" She had moved so quickly that she was round the corner of the building and out of earshot. The three girls looked at one another and shrugged. Julie said that they should try again next day.

The following day in Art class Nomed actually spoke to Rachel, without any cuss words or obscenities. Rachel decided that she should ask her again about the youth group. Nomed wanted to know what they did there. Rachel told her that they usually had someone speak and they would sing and then visit at the end over refreshments. "I don't know if I will come, I might be busy" "Well just let me know and I will come and take you. Where do you live?" "I can come by myself, where is it held." They were actually having a conversation and Nomed found herself liking this bold girl who had broken through her shield of hate and rudeness.

At Rachel's next class she told the others what had happened and they were so happy. They looked for Nomed at break time and invited her to sit with them. She did and Julie used the opportunity to invite her to church on Sunday. Nomed told them that she would never be seen inside a church because God was there and she hated Him. Julie and the others were taken aback but Marie asked her why that was. She said that God had been very cruel to her and her family. Julie asked her what had happened but she said she did not want to talk about it, and said she had to go. The girls looked at one another. They were shocked by Nomed's statement and wondered what could have made her so bitter.

Next Sunday when Julie waited for her friends at the front door of the church building, and was amazed to see Nomed walking towards her. Other kids who were standing around stared at her, because she looked so ...........black. Julie asked if she wanted to come in and sit with her and Nomed's reply was to light up a cigarette. This was just another way Nomed would try to shock people. She refused to go in but continued to stand there until everyone was inside. Marie looked around when she and her mother were sitting down and noticed Nomed had come in and was sitting in the back seat. She smiled to herself, and at the end of the service started to go back and talk to her, but she was gone.

There was no school on Monday but on Tuesday, Rachel found Nomed very talkative. She noticed also that she had her hair tied back from her face and apart from the black lipstick and eye shadow; she was quite a pretty girl. She sat with them again at breaks and made small talk. The girls were careful not to ask her any personal questions, so their time was quite cordial. On Wednesday they reminded her about youth group and she said she would come. Marie's mother was working late so Marie had stayed with Julie and when they arrived there was Nomed. She came in and sat at the back. All went well during the singing. She read the words but didn't sing. Then Brother Bob stood up and he and his wife sang. Nomed became very agitated and got up and ran out. Marie went after her but she took off along the street very quickly. Brother Bob has noticed her leaving and wanted to know who she was. The girls told him that it was a friend from school.

Marie's dad finally arrived home, amid tears and smiles. Marie and her mom were so happy to see him at last. He had lost weight and they were worried but he said that it was because of army food. He was not going to let anything mar this homecoming. He had been told that his term of service was over for the present. He did say however that he was leaving again the following week to see one of his men, but after that he would be home for good. They were so happy, Marie stayed home from school and her mom was able to get the week off. They took turns just sitting by him, sometimes not even talking, just feeling him close and knowing that he was alright.

# BOBBY

He was certainly a different person. He played ball with Marie in the driveway, and teased her about boys. Marie really liked this new dad. He just acted as if he was glad to be home and that he was alive. He asked them if it would be all right if he prayed with them. They could have cried. He asked them if they would go to church with him. He had written the address of the church down somewhere in his baggage. The week was great and when Sunday came, they got ready to go with their dad to whatever church he wanted to go to. They laughed when he drove up to their church. He was surprised when people already knew his wife and daughter. Then he discovered that they had already been coming to services there. The pastor knew that Marie's dad was due home so he made a point of talking to him before he left. The pastor's brother also came and threw his arms around him. Then Marie and her mother realized that the captain Peter had been talking about was her dad. Peter was invited over to visit that afternoon, and they just talked and talked about how real God was. They shed some tears together and they were unashamed. It was obvious that they had had an experience, which had truly bonded them. Peter told Marie's mother over and over what a wonderful person he was. She felt somewhat left out; that was a part of her husband's life, which she was not privy to. She kept her thoughts to herself. The pastor came by to pick Peter up for supper and was invited in. He told the two men how glad he was that God had kept them safe. He asked Marie's mother how she was doing and she started to cry. Everyone was looking at her not really knowing what was wrong, and then the pastor said that he was going to pray and I suppose give Marie's mother time to compose herself, not wanting to embarrass her. When he started to pray however, Marie's mother started to sob. Marie and her dad moved closer to her and the pastor closed his prayer. He was going to leave quietly with Peter but Marie's mom told him that she was suddenly overwhelmed by the conviction of sin and needed to have God's forgiveness in her life. The pastor prayed again and then shook her hand and then her husband's and left with Peter.

They spent the rest of the day talking about God, and the Lord Jesus and Marie's dad told about his experience in the middle of the battlefield. It was even more poignant to Marie as she realized that the story, which Peter had told them, was her father's story too. The soldier that he was going to visit was the one who had saved his life. Marie's dad kept hugging her mom and saying that they would serve God together. She just nodded and cried some more. Marie had never seen them so happy. At church that night, they went and talked to the pastor about becoming members. Everything seemed to be working out perfectly for Marie's parents.

Next day at school, Nomed was back to her usual insolent self. At break time when the girls tried to talk to her, she was very hostile. "You guys are all religious freaks, just leave me alone. I hate God." Later in the afternoon, they tried to talk to her again. She screamed at them so they backed off and left her alone. That night Julie talked to her dad and he suggested that perhaps it would be better if just one person talked to her. Nomed did not turn up to school on Tuesday and the girls were worried that she was ill. However, on Wednesday, she was back and Rachel asked her during class if she would come that night to youth group. "You never give up. Do you? I do not know. I do not like the leader. He reminds me of someone." "Oh, he is a wonderful person. You would really like him. Please come again. You'll see." " I might come, I'll see"

That night Nomed was there waiting when everyone showed up. She nodded to some of the young people who shouted "Hi". Again, she sat in the back row. Brother Bob started by asking his wife to come and sing with him. They sang a song about the love of God. Julie was sitting beside Nomed and smiled when she heard her say," They sound like angels". By the end of the song, Nomed was crying. Julie gave her a tissue but it was useless. Her black mascara was running down her face and she looked grotesque. Marie leaned over and asked her what was wrong. Nomed was sobbing still. Brother Bob introduced the speaker, an older man who was a member of the church, and then came and sat at the end of the row where the girls were sitting. Marie asked Nomed if she wanted to go to the restroom, so she could wash her face. She agreed and stood up and followed Marie along the row.

Brother Bob stood to let them past, but when Nomed reached him she hesitated not wanting anyone to see her in this mess. He said, "Are you going to be alright?" Nomed lifted her head and suddenly she recognized his face. "Bobby" she whispered. He was taken aback but he said, "Yes, I'm Bobby, Do I know you?" She whispered in an almost inaudible voice, "I'm Ruthie". Brother Bob turned quite pale. His mind was racing. "Ruthie, my Ruthie!" She nodded. He grabbed her and cried almost as hard as Nomed. The girls looked at one another shrugging. No one knew what was going on. They slipped out and went to a little conference room at the back of the building. "Oh Ruthie I thought I had lost you forever, I tried so hard to find you. Where have you been?" When Nomed found her voice she asked him if he really looked for her, and he told her that for years he had tried to get in touch with her. He asked her where she lived and said she must come and visit with his family. He was visibly shaken and at the end of the meeting, when Anna and the girls came looking for them and heard the news they were all amazed.

Anna said she must come home with them, and offered to go and pick up anything she needed from her home. She stroked Nomed's face and said that God had indeed blessed them. She had prayed daily that God would bring this girl to them and heal the wound in her husband's heart. Nomed said that she would like to go with them. The girls were a little overwhelmed by the whole thing. They were extremely glad that they had persisted in inviting their schoolmate to youth group. Nomed had finally stopped crying and her face was washed and clean. She left with Anna and Brother Bob. In the car she broke down again. "Why did you let them take me away?" she sobbed. Bobbie was heartbroken. He was too emotional to explain how he had tried to stop them. When they arrived home, an older woman in a wheel chair met them in the hall. "The babe is asleep" She looked at Bobbie with a question in her eyes. Bobbie explained to her that this was Ruthie, her granddaughter. What rejoicing there was in Bobby's home that night? They just could not believe that God had answered their prayers and that she had just turned up. Ruthie felt very strange, like she was looking at someone else. It didn't seem real.

# CHAPTER THIRTEEN

Bobby and Ruthie sat up for hours talking after Anna and Grandma had gone to bed. He wanted to know everything she done and everywhere she had been. He was horrified when he heard what had happened in her life. He would just hold his head in grief when she told him of the many foster homes and the cried when she told him about the couple who adopted her. Her adopted father had molested her, and when his wife found out she was back in the system again. She had lived in group homes from then on. Finally he showed her where to sleep. Anna had pajamas and a robe on the bed for her. Ruthie slept hard when she finally succumbed to sleep. What a day it had been! When she woke and looked outside she saw flowers in the window box outside the window. The furniture was white and the walls were pale green with a border of flowers and butterflies around the top. The room was so pretty, so different from the place where she lived, a group home where the walls were all beige, the utility furniture was scuffed and broken from the many scuffles between the young people in the home. Most of the youth there were very angry at something or someone in his or her lives. "How could Bobby be living here when she lived in such an awful place? Where was Lillie? Where was her Mother? Where was her Dad? Where had a grandmother come from? She didn't know she had a grandmother. She had so many questions. She stayed for a long time afraid to end the dream. She was sure that once outside the door of this room, she would find herself back in her nightmare life. It was nearly ten o'clock when Anna gently knocked on her door. She expected that someone would come in like they did at the group home, but Anna just knocked again. Nomed walked over and opened the door to find Anna standing there with a tray of breakfast. "I was sure you would be hungry, just let me know if there is anything else you need." Nomed looked at the tray in amazement. She had never had breakfast brought to her room before. She felt like royalty or something. "Thank you, this is great" The words were strange to her, but Anna was so sweet and loving. She asked her if she had slept well, and if she was warm enough, and then left her to eat. "Come on out when you are ready. There is someone who wants to meet you"

Nomed hurried through her breakfast, wondering who 'the somebody' was. She slipped out still in her nightclothes, and came face to face with the sweetest little girl she had ever seen. Her tousled blonde curls and her sky blue eyes made her look like a cherub. Momentarily Nomed thought she was in heaven then remembered quickly that she probably would never go there. The little girl said "Hi!" Nomed smiled and walked with her to the living room where everyone sat waiting. "I see Ruth-Ann has already introduced herself." Ruth-Ann hurried off and brought back a doll. Nomed took it from her and Ruth-Ann promptly took it back. Everyone laughed, and Anna explained that Ruth-Ann wanted her to play but had not learned to share yet. Joy was seen in all their faces. Nomed didn't ever remember being anywhere where there was so much joy. It seemed to fill the house. She thought about where she lived and suddenly remembered that she had not kept her curfew. She would be in big trouble, not that being in trouble was new to her, but she would lose her privileges. She told them that she would have to go and explain why she did not go home the previous night. "Can you come and explain so I don't lose my room. I hate having to share." Anna rose from her chair and quickly exclaimed that she would call and explain what had happened and that Nomed could stay with them if she liked. "I can't or they will give my room to someone else" "I mean forever sweetie" "You mean leave the group home. I wouldn't have to back there."

Nomed could not hold back the tears. "Oh thank you, thank you"

# BOBBY

Grandma wheeled herself over and reached to give Nomed a hug. "So Missy, why do you call yourself Nomed, That is a strange name, is it because you have wandered around so much?" "No its Nomed, N O M E D and well it's because, I well, sometime ago I was told that I was a demon so I decided to be one. I decided to call myself Demon. The people at the shelter would not let me so I just changed the letters around. It sounds kind of stupid now." "I prefer Ruthie so that's what I'm going to call you "said Grandma in her matter of fact way. She had long since stopped standing on ceremony.

Nomed told Grandma that she would like that, because she didn't want to be Nomed anymore. Bobby who had left the room came back and announced that Nomed had been released for a week but that in the meantime they could sign all the necessary papers so she could leave the home for good. Ruthie hugged her big brother, thanking him over and over. "What would you like to do for the rest of the day? Tomorrow you are expected back at school but you are off the hook for today". She didn't know what she wanted to do. She wanted to believe what was happening to her was true and that was taking up most of her thoughts.

Just then Ruthann wandered in and gave Ruthie a doll. Ruthie looked around; she didn't quite know what to do with the doll. Then Ruthann put out her hand and took it back. Everyone laughed. Anna told her that Ruthann was just showing her the doll and that she had not learned to share. "She's not the only one!" Ruthie blurted out. She watched the happy smiling child and was amazed that no one was making her stay in a certain place. She was allowed to make as much noise as she wanted to. She would point to the TV and someone would put music for her and she would dance. Ruthie could not believe that life could be so well so utterly devoid of stress or friction. She pinched herself several times that day just to make sure she was not dreaming. Happiness just seemed to fill that house.

After dinner while they were eating their apple pie, Ruthie was

44

quite overtaken with sobbing. Bobby was quickly at her side. "What is it Ruthie. What can I do?" Ruthie cried inconsolably for a few moments then managed to say that the pie reminded her of her mother. Bobby hugged her very tight and wept himself. He knew that they needed to talk about many things so he sent a quick signal to Anna, and she took everyone to another room. Bobby and Ruthie talked for a very long time. Anna came back once and said that they were leaving for church. They were still talking when everyone returned, two hours later.

"Everyone was asking where you were and if you were all right. Pastor wanted to know what you were doing. I told him about God bringing Ruthie home and he is so happy for you." Ruthie heard the word *home* and was soon sobbing again. She was emotionally exhausted after talking to Bobbie and really wanted to lie down but she was a little afraid that everything would disappear if she did. Anna asked her if she wanted to go to bed and have her hot chocolate there or come and sit with them. Ruthie opted to stay with the others. She went to the family room and looked longingly at the piano. Grandma asked her if she wanted to play and she quickly shook her head. Would you like to learn? You could have lessons. Ruthie told her that she didn't know. Grandma had a very sad look in her eyes. She could tell that Ruthie had been through the mill, and would need a lot of love to help her feel better. She wheeled herself over and leaned forward to give Ruthie a hug. Ruthie was unaccustomed to such advances and had a questioning look on her face. Grandma asked her if she could have a hug, and Ruthie squeezed her tight. Grandma whispered in her ear that she loved her and was so glad that God had brought her home.

In the kitchen Anna had told Bobby that Rachel and Julie had been worried about Nomed. She had explained that Nomed was really Bobby's little sister who had been lost for years and that her name was really Ruthie. Bobby decided to call and thank the girls for bringing Ruthie to church the previous day. Anna went off to put Ruthann to bed and Bobby brought the hot chocolate in to Ruthie and Grandma. He asked Ruthie if she was ready to go back to school and if she wanted to ride with him on his way to work. "I still work at the hardware store; do you remember the one we passed on the way to school?" "You do! I wish I had known that I could have found you". He hugged her again and this time she felt more relaxed to him. He somehow felt responsible for all the awful things, which had happened to her and wanted so much to make things up to her. She had gone through her clothes and didn't really like any of them anymore. She decided on a sweater and a pair of jeans, which Anna had given her.

Ruthie was awestruck by the reaction of her schoolmates. Rachel, Julie and Marie had warned most of their friends to take it easy on her, so they greeted her with "Hi," and "Hello" and "Missed you yesterday" She found herself responding with a smile. It was strange for her but she rather liked it. It made her feel that her schoolmates actually could like her and that was a miracle. The four girls chatted when they had opportunity and she found herself enjoying her day. Her new friends asked her if she wanted to come by after school and she told them she would ask Anna when she got home. After she had said that she questioned herself, about what was happening to her. When was the last time she had even thought of asking permission. Her friends did not blink an eye, or give the impression that they thought she was lame in doing it. In fact they said that they would walk round to where she now lived and call to see if she could go with them. She thanked them. Again she wondered where the words came from. She felt different and she liked it.

She had told Rachel that she wanted to be called Ruth and Rachel had passed the message on. Soon most of her classmates were doing the same. The teachers had noticed the change as well. It was all the buzz in the teacher's lounge. They were asking each other what had happened to Nomed to make such a change in her. One teacher said that it was nothing short of a miracle. They all agreed. Little did they know how true that was. They were informed that she was calling her-self Ruth and they agreed that the new name suited her new look.

After school Bobby picked her up and dropped her off. She asked him about going out with her friends, and he told her that it would be wonderful and that she should invite them to come anytime to hang out. He said that she should let Anna know so she wouldn't worry but that she could go where she pleased. She told Anna, and got the same response. Grandma wheeled herself over and gave her a hug. "I love you child, I am so glad you are here. I would like to take you shopping tomorrow, if that is alright with you" Ruthie grinned. "I would love to. I need to find some new clothes." Anna smiled to herself. "God is good," she thought, and silently gave thanks to her Heavenly father for bringing Ruthie home.

She told Ruthie that they would eat at 6:30 when Bobby came home but she could call if she was going to be late and they would keep a plate for her. It wasn't long until her friends were at the door. Anna invited them in to meet Grandma and Ruthann who had just awak-ened from her nap. They ended up having so much fun with her that it was time for them to go home. They planned to come the following afternoon and go to the park. "Do you have a bicycle?" Helen asked. "No!" she said, shaking her head slowly. "Don't worry. We will walk" They left slowly waving goodbye to Ruthann and blowing her kisses. "See you tomorrow."

Anna lost no time in telling Bobby that Ruthie needed a bicycle so she could ride with her friends and his reaction puzzled her. She touched his arm and asked if he was all right. He told her that he had determined a long time ago that he was going to buy a bicycle for his two sisters but never could. He would be so glad to be able to buy Ruthie a bicycle, but he would like to take her to the store to pick it out. Anna smiled sweetly and gave her husband a hug. She had prom-ised herself that come the weekend she was going to invite Ruthie to go shopping for new clothes. She had noticed that when Ruthie wore her black clothes she seemed uncomfortable, so she wanted to renew her wardrobe if Ruthie agreed. She told Bobbie and he was in full agreement.

The next weekend they all went to the mall and Ruthie was really excited when Anna invited her into a clothes shop and told her to pick out something to wear. Ruthie told her that she had already done enough. Anna told her it was a welcome home present so she consented and Anna showed her some pretty tops in blue and peach. She chose the blue but lingered at the buttercup yellow, and a navy one before making up her mind. Anna went over and making sure that they were the right size placed them both on the counter. They moved to the slacks and Anna showed her a couple of styles, and told her to go try them on. She tried a navy, beige and a charcoal grey. When she tried them on, the beige one didn't fit. Anna told her to bring the other two and she could have them both. Next Anna had her choose a dress, then shoes. She couldn't believe how she looked in a dress. It had been a long time since she had worn one. They had to go to another store for the shoes. They went home after buying the shoes because Ruthann was getting restless and needed her nap.

At home Ruthie tried on and modeled her new clothes. Bobby told her that she looked pretty but that she needed to put on her jeans and come with him because he was going to the store to get her a bicycle. She was thrilled, and was ready in a blink. But just then Ruthann who had been following her around came staggering in Ruthie's long black boots. Bobbie grinned at her "Hi Bootsie!" he said laughing. They all laughed. Somehow in a strange way it made Ruthie feel as if she belonged. Soon after she and Bobby left for the store to get her bicycle. He asked her how she was feeling, sensing that there was a lot he didn't know about the time they had been separated. She was emotional as she answered and told him that she still felt as if she was dreaming. "Me too, Sis, Me too. If only we could find Lillie my life would be complete" "Did they take her the same time as they took me?"

They talked all the way to the store and back. When they arrived back home they sat in the car still talking. Ruthie had started to open up about her experiences and Bobby wanted her to be able to continue without interruption. She told him that she had been to six different foster homes and then a couple that lived close to the state border, on an isolated farm agreed to adopt her. Her new mother, Rebecca worked in the nearest village and left for work each day before Ruthie got home from school. Steve her new father would pick her up from school and play with her. Rebecca would have their supper all ready, and after they ate they would wash up the dishes and watch TV or play board games. She was so happy at first, and then things got a little weird. Steve would sit on her bed and rub her back until she went to sleep just like Lilly would do when she was scared. Then one night he put his hand under her clothes. She didn't like it and she told him to stop. He told her not to worry, that it was ok, that it was just something people did when they loved one another. She had let him continue, and as the days went on she was more and more unhappy about it.

Ruthie had asked her mother if she could stay up until her she came home from work and her mother agreed, but when she came home she was so tired that she would fall asleep in the armchair. Steve would still put her to bed and do things, which made her uncomfortable. Life was like that for a long time, and then on her thirteenth birthday Steve told her that now she was a grownup they could really love one another like grownups. That night it hurt so bad that she cried out for her mother, Rebecca, but she did not come. The next day she started her period and didn't know why she was bleeding, and was very scared and thought she was going to die. Rebecca was making cookies and brought one to her. Ruthie had blurted out to her that she was bleeding to death because Steve had hurt her. Rebecca was horrified, and started asking her what had happened.

When Ruthie told her she asked her more questions and soon knew the whole story. She was incensed, hugged Ruthie and called the police.

It was like the day that her mother died. Social workers came and took Ruthie away. She stayed in a state home for a week then a halfway house, and then her mother came and talked to her and told her that she couldn't keep her anymore because she was getting a divorce and leaving the farm. She couldn't afford her any more and she was sorry. The social workers moved her again so she would not be near that area, and told her it was for her own safety. That was when she moved to the youth home and had lived there ever since. Bobby was distraught; his little sister had suffered so much, and he could not understand why God had allowed this to happen. He chided himself, wondering what more he could have done to search for her. He hugged her and told her that he loved her and would always take care of her. That sounded very good to Ruthie. She told Bobbie that she wasn't sure if he really wanted her in his home when she had been so bad. He told her that she had done nothing wrong, that her adopting father had not loved her but had used and abused her and that she should never feel that she was unwanted again. They clung to each other and continued to just sit in the car until they saw Grandma wheeling herself out the door coming towards them. "Are you two going to sit there all night?"

They climbed out and went inside with her, to find Ruthann still walking around in her boots. Anna saw that they had been crying and scooped Ruthann up and left the room calling Grandma to come. "I am so sorry you had to suffer so. I had always hoped that you would be somewhere happy like Lillie. She was in a very happy home and did not really want to leave. Things were so much better for her there than at our home." "I used to think of you all, my three brothers and Lillie all living happy somewhere with Mom. I wasn't sure what happened to her, all I knew was that Dad left. Oh Bobby I have been so mean to everyone, at the home, at school, to my teachers and to all the kids. You have no idea. That was why they called me a demon. I want things to be different now. I want to be a better person but I don't know how." Bobby asked her if she would mind if he prayed with her. She told him that it was all right. Bobby thanked God for uniting them once more, and asked God to bring peace to Ruthie's heart. He knew that only God himself could erase the anguish of the things, which had happened to her and wished in his heart for a bigger miracle that God would reveal himself to her in a saving way.

By suppertime Ruthie had washed her face and looked better and sat down to play with Ruthann. She was such a sweet child and her love was so unconditional. She would wrap her arms around Ruthie's neck and plant a very wet kiss on her face. It was like a balm to Ruthie's troubled heart. They played together for an hour, rocking teddy bears and dolls to sleep, until it was Ruthann's bedtime. "Thank you, you just wore her out. She should sleep well tonight." said Anna. "I think I will too" replied Ruthie with a faint smile.

Anna sailed off to put Ruthann to bed and Grandma said that she was going to bed early to read. Bobby asked if Ruthie wanted to watch a movie or play a game or something. She said that what she really wanted was for him to help her think of a way that she could let all of the kids she knew how sorry she was that she had been so awful to them. She also wanted to know more about God and His Son and what He had done to deserve to die. She had thought that she deserved to die but she didn't think that God's son would have done anything wrong. Bobby explained to her that Jesus, God's son had never sinned his whole life but that He had been born so that He would die for His people, and pay the price for all their sin. Ruthie wanted to know why anyone would want to do that for people he didn't even know. Bobby explained that God knows everyone, and planned that Jesus would die for His people before he even made the world. Ruthie was hungry for more information about this wonderful person and Bobby was only too grateful to have the opportunity to tell her. Anna came back and sat down to listen. She always loved to hear Bobby talk about the Lord. His face always glowed when he spoke about the Lord Jesus. She was so proud to have him as her husband. Ruthie suddenly asked, "Are you one of God's children, and are you?" turning to Anna. "We are." said Bobby. Ruthie was crying again, "I want to be too; how can I become God's child?" Bobby went and kneeled before her and took her hand and prayed and asked God to make it clear to Ruthie. He tried to explain about conviction and repentance, and before long realized that God was indeed bringing about a change in his sister's heart. Before they went to bed that night Ruthie experienced the miracle of salvation through the finished work of the Lord Jesus. She was a changed girl. She wanted to tell everyone in church next day. Julie was the first person she met and she was so happy. Bobbie told his pastor that God had saved Ruthie and the pastor shook his hand warmly "More than you can ask or think, Brother" Bobby nodded his head in agreement. "You are right. God gives more abundantly."

On the way home Bobby asked Ruthie if she would be willing to tell her story to the young people at the youth group. She said that she would think about it but thought that she would be nervous to talk in front of anyone. She talked to her grandmother when they got home. Grandma told her she would be fine, that she was a strong person, and that she could do anything she wanted to do. She said that all these years of unhappiness had been God seasoning her for His work. Ruthie looked at her and thought about that for a while. She thought that if all that she had gone through had been for God's purpose then it was all worthwhile. If God had given her the strength to go through those hardships then she could tell the other young people about it. She told Bobby she would talk to the young people.

The night came and Bobby introduced her as his sister. He said that they had been separated by circumstances a long time ago and that she was going to tell them her story. She stood up and said. This is not really my story. It is God's story. She then told them about being taken from her home and sent to one foster care family after another. She went to six of them in five years, and then was adopted, at last, by a couple that sounded as if they really wanted her. She told them that her adopted father had hurt her and she spent the rest of her life in a group home. That was until God used some of the girls from the youth group to persuade her to come to church. There she had not only found her brother but also the Lord. Jesus Christ. The young people were transfixed. No one took his or her eyes of her while she was speaking. She ended by telling them that she was forever grateful to her friends for inviting her to come to a place where she was able to unite with her beloved brother and grandmother and to God for inviting her into the family of God. . She sat down and Anna who was sitting at the piano started playing. She looked across at Bobby and he went over and the two of them sang that wonderful old hymn written by William T Sleeper, in 1887.

"Out of my bondage, sorrow and night,
Jesus I come. Jesus I come
Into thy freedom, gladness and light,
Jesus I come to Thee
Out of my sickness, into Thy health
Out of my want and into thy wealth
Out of my sin and into Thyself.
Jesus I come to Thee.
Out of shameful failure and loss,
Jesus I come Jesus I come
Into the glorious gain of Thy cross
Jesus I come to Thee
Out of earth's sorrows, into thy balm
Out of life's storms and into Thy calm,
Out of distress to jubilant Psalm,
Jesus I come to Thee.
Out of unrest and arrogant pride,
Jesus I come Jesus I come,
Into Thy blessed will to abide,

Jesus I come to Thee.
Out of myself to dwell in Thy love,
Out of despair into raptures above.
Upward for aye on wings like a dove.
Jesus I come to Thee."

Then Bobby went to the front and started to speak. He said that he had tried everything in his power to find his sister when they were separated, but was unable to find her. He had prayed that God would reunite them some day. He admitted that sometimes he almost gave up hope of that ever happening, when one day out of the blue, God just brought Ruthie in through the door of the very church he was in. God is the miracle worker. Jesus is the Good Shepherd, watching out for His sheep and when the time is right He draws them into His fold. He told them that there were many dangers in the world and a multitude of pitfalls, but that the Good Shepherd knew all about them. Just as the shepherd goes out looking for the sheep which gets lost and embraces and carries it back to the safety of the fold, Jesus seeks out His children, no matter where they are, and brings them into the family of God, embraces them and loves them. Bobby read Isaiah 53 from the King James Version of the Bible. "Jesus was wounded for our transgressions and bruised for our iniquities. The chastisement of our peace was upon Him and with His stripes we are healed. All we like sheep have gone astray, we have turned everyone to his own way and God has laid on Him the iniquity of us all." Paul the great Apostle said in Acts 20 that grievous wolves would enter among God's children and tear them apart. God made preparation for this by sending His Son to die on the cross for the sins of His people. Bobby then quoted Second Corinthians, "All things are of God, who hath reconciled us to himself by Christ Jesus, and hath given to us the ministry of reconciliation, to wit, that God was in Christ, reconciling the world to himself, not imputing their trespasses unto them." In other words, Bobby said, "God has already forgiven you in Christ for all the sins and wrongdoing that you have ever been involved with. Christ has suffered the shame and death for you. If you come to Him in repentance before God, then you will be truly free."

There was a hush over the entire group when Bobbie finished speaking. Many hearts were touched. Several of the young people came to Bobby after ward to ask questions. There was a sense of excitement among the young people. The pastor looked in at one point and joined with bobby helping to answer some of the questions. He had brought his brother with him and had wanted to talk to Bobby. He soon realized that a work of the Spirit of God was going on and he stayed to pray with one or two of the young men. No one wanted to leave; such was the warmth felt by all. Some of the young people had been more deeply involved in sin than the others but all felt the need for God's forgiveness.

When everyone had gone, Bobby at last had time to tell his little sister how thankful he was that she had agreed to speak that night. He told her that she had been used of God to speak to the hearts of many of the young people. He himself felt so blessed to have been in the position where God could use him. It was something, which he prayed for everyday. The pastor told him that he would like a few words so he told Anna to go on home as it was late and that he would get a ride. He knew that Anna did not like to be too late in case Ruthann was acting up with Grandma. He saw them off and then turned to the pastor. They prayed together for the young people and asked God for guidance for them as new Christians. Peter, pastor's brother, told him that his friend 'Slow Joe' was being released from the hospital and as he had no family Peter had invited him to come and live there. He was going to find an apartment and they would be roommates until Joe was back on his feet. He wondered if Bobby could use some help with the young people's group. He felt that it would help Joe recuperate, if he could help other people. Peter told him that when he and his captain went back to visit Joe in the hospital he had told him about the young people's group and he wanted to know if he could join in when he got there. Bobby was thrilled. He had hoped that perhaps Peter would help him, just because he was always a little rushed on Wednesdays, getting from the hardware store to home and then to the church building. His captain had stayed with Joe and was traveling back with him. Peter had come on ahead to find the apartment and also because he had an interview for a job.

Ruthie was glowing. She felt like a new person. Everyday was a new opportunity for her to do something for the Lord. She asked Anna to help her with her makeup. She was so finished with her 'black' look. She told Anna "I'm in the light now" She went around the house singing "Out of the darkness into your light, Jesus I come Jesus I come" "You have a beautiful voice; you will have to sing for us in church some day." "Do you think I could?" "Come I will play for you and you sing" Anna sat down at the piano and Ruthie hummed along, reading the words from the music. It was an old hymn written by Thoro Harris in 1931. Then she started to sing. Her voice sounded like an angel. She was concentrating on the words and didn't hear Grandma and Bobby come into the room.

Who can cheer the heart like Jesus?
By His presence all divine?
True and tender, pure and precious,
O how blest to call Him mine.
Love of Christ so freely given,
Grace of God beyond degree,
Mercy higher than the heaven.
Deeper than the deepest sea.
What a wonderful redemption.
Never can a mortal know.
How my sin, though red like crimson,

Can be whiter than the snow.
Every need my God supplying.
Every good in Him I see;
On His strength divine relying.
He is all in all to me,
By the crystal flowing river,
With the ransomed I will sing,
And forever and forever
Praise and glorify the king.
All that thrills my soul is Jesus,
He is more than life to me;
And the fairest of ten thousand,
In my blessed Lord I see.

As she sang there were tears in her eyes. These words although written so long ago were straight from her heart. She turned and saw Bobby and Grandma, and there were tears in their eyes too. They were so glad she was in their lives again but gladder that Christ was in hers. God had given so many blessings to them both. Grandma thought about the first time she met Bobby when she was still in the nursing home. She knew he was special that day and since then he had become very precious. His joys were her joys. She felt that she had begun to live again when he entered her life and when God saved him he showed by his life that he was a chosen vessel for his Lord. Anna's face glowed, when she turned from the piano. "That was beautiful Ruthie; I think we have a new soloist in our youth group." Grandma turned and wheeled herself towards the bedrooms. "Off to bed Grandma?" said Bobby. "Yes" she answered but it was with a sob. Bobby quickly was by her side giving her a hug. "You ok" "Do you think God could ever forgive my son for what he did?" Bobbie put his arms around her and held her close. He could not begin to know the anguish that her son's actions had brought her. He told her that when God sent His Son to die for sinners, it meant that all kinds of sin would be forgiven. "We just need to forgive him ourselves, and not worry about whether God can forgive. He forgave those who put Him to death. Jesus asked His Father to forgive them." it was small consolation to Grandma, and she went off to bed with a heavy heart.

Anna and Bobbie prayed together that night, and asked for peace for Grandma. She was such a sweet lady and they knew her heart was heavy with the burden of what her son had done. Bobby confided to Anna that he did have misgivings when he thought of his father. He wondered how he would react if he ever met him. He knew that some-day that could happen and asked God for the grace it would take for him to accept him or even want to speak to him. He kissed Anna and was soon asleep, dreaming of Lillie and his Dad.

# CHAPTER FOURTEEN

Marie and her mother were really excited; her dad had been told that his term of service was over and when he got home he had three weeks before he started back to his old job again. Marie had a new song in her heart since the night she became a Christian. Life would be so different now. All three members of her family were now Christians, and would be going to church together. They received a call from her Dad, and as she listened to her mother's end of the conversation, she was pacing the floor. Her mother laughed at her and told her to go pick up another phone so she could listen in. He was on his way home and was actually bringing someone with him. The guy who had saved his life was coming with him and another buddy of theirs was going to have an apartment ready for him when they arrived. He asked if he could come over sometimes to visit and have dinner. That was new for them because they never ever had people over before. Marie's mother readily agreed.

When they finally got off the phone and started making plans for his homecoming, the phone rang again. It was Carla. She was bubbling over with excitement. She was going to be a bridesmaid. Her sister was getting married. Her dress was going to be lavender, her favorite color. "She is getting married to the guy I told you about, the one who was in prison. She said that even after all the quarrelling with her parents Paula still insisted that she loved him. They were horrified that Paula, who had always caused them a certain amount of grief, was about to marry someone who had been in prison. He had no job and was having difficulty finding one because of his history and he just seemed to be always hanging about. Her father had sat him down one day with the intention of telling him to get lost but after talking to him decided that he liked the young guy and decided to give him a break and hire him. He started him in the mailroom, and he had done so well that he had been promoted three times before the end of his first year. Meantime Paula had buckled down and finished all her classes and was graduating. She asked her dad if she could work for him and her dad agreed, although he thought that it was probably her boyfriend who was the draw rather than he. She worked a few days now and then and discovered that her dad and her boyfriend had become buddies. He had given his consent for them to be married, and then he was going to be sending him to do some courses in the training center, which was right there, and she was coming with them. She wanted to stay with Marie because well they would be on their honeymoon and she didn't want to be a third wheel. She had hardly taken a breath the whole time. Marie said that of course she could stay with them. She also told Carla that she had become a Christian and asked if she would come to church with her. Carla didn't answer right away and Marie asked if she was still there. Carla told her that that was most amazing because she and her sister and her sister's boyfriend were all Christians and would love to go with them. She asked if it was Julie's dad's church and was so excited to know that it was. When they hung up Marie told her that Carla was coming for the whole summer and that was only two weeks away. She called Julie and Rachel to tell them that Carla was coming for the whole summer, and staying with her, and that she was a Christian too. It was amazing. Julie was not home so she told her mother. Her mother said that Julie was with her uncle. They were working on the apartment, which her uncle was moving into. Julie and her dad were helping to clean and paint it. It was near the hospital where Marie's mother worked. Joe was still going to need treatments and checkups so it would be convenient for him. Marie asked her mother if she knew where the Shafer Institute of business was because that is where Carla's sister would be staying. Marie's mother knew one of the instructors. She said that the courses there were intense. They did eight-week courses but they were actually full year college courses. Everyone who went there had to prove himself or herself by doing their first year of college by correspondence. Paula's boyfriend had obviously stayed the course so must not be too bad. They had to live in and their whole life was work; work; work.

Marie's mother remembered that Paula was quite rebellious as a teenager and hoped that she would settle into this difficult life. She thought to herself that it was not a great start to any marriage. She really hoped it would work out for them. However she had other things to think about. Her husband was coming home. He had become so serious in the last few years, become quieter and less talkative. Now he couldn't stop. She was excited. Life would be better. She called the hospital and arranged to have the week off after her husband arrived home. Marie was making a poster to put up to welcome her dad home. They put streamers up as well. She called the pastor to see if he wanted to come by and visit. He still wasn't home, but she talked to his wife and she said that they would come.

Next day dawned bright and beautiful. Marie asked her principal if she could go home early because her dad was coming home and he consented. They were getting out early that day anyway so it would be no problem. Her mother came and picked her up, and found her with Julie, Rachel and Ruthie. "We had an unexpected half day." "Hop in and I will drive you home." "Thanks." No sooner had they set off than Marie's mother got a call from her dad. He had arrived at the base and needed picked up. Marie's mother told them she would drop them at her home and take them home later if that was all right. While she waited for her parents Marie told the girls all about Carla and her sister Paula. They started planning all kinds of adventures. "You guys are really cool friends." said Ruthie. "We do have a lot of fun together."

Marie's dad finally arrived and all the girls welcomed him in. His friend Joe stood back. He was thinking how nice it would be to be welcomed home like that. After all the handshakes and hugs Marie's dad turned to Joe and said, "Come on in. This is my wife Sherri and my daughter Marie. She will have to introduce the others. Marie shook hands with Joe and thanked him for helping her dad. He brushed off the complement. Marie introduced him to Julie, Rachel and Ruthie. He shook hands with everyone and said, "I had a sister called Ruthie" "I thought you had no family." "I lost them all a long time ago" "Oh I am sorry" "Come sit down." "I'll take you home now" said Sherri. "Oh its ok, my brother is coming and will take us home." "And my dad is coming for me". He wants to meet Joe and I think Peter is coming to pick up Joe." Just at that moment someone knocked the door. Marie opened it and invited Bobby in. He shook hands with Marie's dad then turned to Joe. Joe had stood up and was staring at Bobbie. "Bobby. It can't be. Are you Bobbie, my brother?" Bobby, suddenly recognizing his older brother was speechless. The tears welled up and then Joe turned around and said "Ruthie Are you my little sister?" Bobby getting over his shock, grabbed Joe but Joe cried out in pain. "I am so sorry" "I had no idea. I… Please forgive me" Joe shook his head. "It's all right. It is just still a bit tender back there. Let me hug you instead and come here little Ruthie. Am I glad to see you?" A few minutes later Julie's dad arrived with Peter.

The comrades were glad to be reunited and when Peter found out that Joe and Bobby were brothers his joy knew no bounds. He had felt so sorry for his friend because he had no one to call family and he had such a loving one. Now his friend had a family too. What a joy! Bobby too was elated. He had newfound confidence that God would reunite his whole family one-day and hoped that it would be soon. Marie's mother was bewildered. Her dad explained that Peter was the other army buddy whose life had been saved by Joe. Bobby then told them that Joe was his long lost brother whom he hadn't seen in ten years. Ruth was sobbing for joy. Joe wiped his eyes and looked around again. "So you and Peter know one another?" "Yes, we go to the same church"

Joe just shook his head in disbelief. "How good is God? He does things when you least expect them." Marie's dad suddenly broke out in song, very uncharacteristically, "What a day of rejoicing that will be; when we all see Jesus. We'll sing and shout the victory" His wife hugged him. No one wanted to leave. Bobby asked Joe to come home with him.

He looked at Peter and he said "We pay by the month, so if you want to go home with your brother that would be ok" Joe hugged Bobby again but told him that he would spend a while with Peter until he figured out what he needed to do about his health. Peter told him that the apartment was not quite ready so they were actually going to sleep at his brothers for a few days. Joe reconsidered," So if you wouldn't mind, maybe I could stay with Bobby instead." "That would be absolutely fine; we will pick you up tomorrow and take you to the doctor, and get you organized." Pastor asked if he could pray and he thanked God for all the things that had come to pass. Then Bobby took Joe and Ruthie, and Helen and started home, with another over-whelming surprise for Anna and Grandma. They dropped Rachel off at her home and quickly drove home and went inside. "Anna, Grandma, come quickly,"

Anna was at his side in a flash, followed by his mother who had gotten quite speedy on her wheelchair. She turned white when she saw Joe. He looked so much like her son the day he left her forever. Bobby told them that God had sent Joe back to them after all these years. Grandma had realized that he wasn't old enough to be her son, and quickly recovered from her shock. Joe blinked at her. "I even have a grandma. I can't take all this in, who is this?" as Ruthann shyly came around the corner. "This is my wife Anna and my daughter Ruthann and your grandmother." "Where did you find him?" said Anna in bewil-derment. He is the Joe who saved Peter's life" "Oh wow, Can he stay with us?" "For a few days, he and Peter have an apartment but they may change their minds after a while." They sat forever around the supper table talking excitedly, asking question after question. Bobby really wanted to know about his older brother. Joe knew nothing about him. He was interested in finding out more about his grandmother. Anna prepared a room for him, and Bobby helped him get ready for bed. He needed dressings on his back and Bobby was only too glad to help. They all sank into a very restless sleep.

# CHAPTER FIFTEEN

Back at Marie's home, after everyone left Sherri started scurrying around to get supper ready. Her dad sat down on the couch and Marie plopped down beside him. He called Sherrie over. "Come sit by me for a few minutes. I am so glad to be home with my girls." He just sat there with his arms around them and savored the moment. "Aren't you hungry?" asked Sherri. "Yes I'm starving, but I just want to sit here with you. There were many times when I thought I would never see you again." Sherri shuddered, but asked no questions. She knew that when he wanted to tell her about the experience he would. Meantime she was really glad he was back home with her. He then did something unprecedented. He bowed his head and thanked God for bringing them all together again and for bringing all three of them into the family of God. Sherri thought about the day when he was called back into service and how scared she had been. Now she realized that God had orchestrated all of it. She remembered a sermon she had heard recently about God's ways being higher than our ways and His thoughts being above our thoughts. Now she understood. From now on she would seek to find God's purpose in everything. She didn't know very much about the Bible but she was sure of one thing and that was that God was in charge. After they had eaten they just sat there with no TV, talking quietly with one another, so glad that they were all there together.

The last days of school went by very slowly. The girls couldn't wait to see Carla and spend time with her. They were thrilled to know that she too was a Christian. Finally the day arrived and they were all at Marie's home waiting to hear from Carla. She was going to call

when the plane landed. Then Sherri and her husband were going to get
Carla her sister and new brother-in -law. They were all there, Rachel,
Julie and Ruthie. They were so excited when everyone arrived home.
Marie's dad winked at Julie's new husband, and they went into the
kitchen. "Too many women in there" he grinned. They were sitting
having coffee and chatting about the study course he was about to
start, when Bobbie arrived for Ruthie. He was invited into the kitchen
as well. The girls were all talking at once and hadn't even heard him
knocking at the door. He was introduced to Julie's husband, and once
more he was made speechless. Thomas Paula's husband had his hand
outstretched and looked quizzically at Bobby when he didn't respond.
"Tommy, Are you Tommy?" "Yes," said Tommy, "but I don't understand.
Do you know me." "? Do I know you? You are my brother." "Bobby,
Oh my goodness! You are! Bobby I thought I would never see you
again." I can't believe this." Bobby had a difficult time holding on to
his composure. "I am so totally overwhelmed by God's goodness in
answering my prayers, that I have no words" Thomas' heart leapt when
he heard Bobby speak. "Do you know the Lord, too?" he asked. "Yes
oh yes" Bobby answered. He was having difficulty speaking, his joy
was so great. God was answering his prayers more quickly than he
could absorb. Ruthie came in at that point to say there were ready and
frowned when she saw her brother crying like a baby. "What is wrong,
Bobby? Are you ok?" Bobby just pointed at Thomas. Thomas said, "He
is my brother." The realization dawned on Ruthie, "Then you are my
brother too. I'm Ruthie" Thomas jumped up and grabbed Ruthie "Oh
you are all grown up. Has it been this long? How are Mom and Lillie?"
Michael left them knowing that there was a lot of history in this family. They quickly told Thomas about their mother's untimely death and
Thomas chided himself for leaving and not protecting her. They told
him that Joe was at their home and they should go and let him know
that he was here. Paula came in next and heard all the news; she knew
he longed to find his family but was sad for him to find that his mother

was dead. Then they told him about their grandmother. She was going to be surprised again.

Thomas and Paula needed to go and sign in at the college. They had two days to get everything together before starting their studies. Thomas told them that they had no classes at the weekends but would have a lot of homework to do. They would try and find some free time to visit. Bobby drove them to the college and waited while they did their paperwork, got their keys and unloaded their bags into their room. He invited them to come and eat supper and then he would bring them back. Soon they were on their way to see Joe and Grandma. Again they dropped Julie off home and made their way to Bobby's home. The first person they met was Ruthann. Bobby introduced her to them Paula bent down and Ruthann gave her the doll she was carrying. Paula pretended to put the doll to sleep. Ruthann took it back. Anna appeared and was introduced to Paula and Thomas. She shook their hands and smiled. "This is Thomas, Anna, my brother," "You are kidding, No way. I can't believe it" "It is pretty unbelievable, "said Paula. She had discovered another whole family and loved it. We have to call Dad and tell him. Just then Joe wandered in. "We found Tommy." Thomas at once blurted out "I didn't run off with the money I am so sorry I couldn't find you. I didn't get very far when I was mugged. Are you ok? Please forgive me" Joe looked sadly at his brother. I forgave you a long time ago. I am so sorry you are still worrying about that. Besides I would forgive you anything because God has forgiven me" Thomas was overjoyed. Joe didn't hate him, and God had saved him. What a wonderful God to give so many blessing all at one time. Anna told everyone to sit and she went for Grandma. Thomas was weeping but managed to get out the words, "I am Thomas and this is my wife Paula." "Not our Thomas" "Yes our Thomas" Oh come here, I never knew I had such handsome grandchildren. I used to wish for grandchildren and had long since given up hope and now God is raining them down on me.

She hugged Thomas and he didn't want to let go. Bobby looked around the room and thought about how blessed he was and how much God had given him. He was thrilled. Thomas moved over to Joe. "Joe I want you to know that the night I ran off with the money, I just wanted to eat I was so hungry. I was going to bring it back to you. I didn't get very far when three guys attacked me. I lashed out at them and gave them what I wanted to give my father. One of them fell and hit his head. Somebody had seen the fight start and called the police. The police came and the other two boys had taken off and I was arrested. They found the money and thought I had stolen it from him. When they heard that I had no job and no address they threw me in jail. The guy, who had fallen, took the money but told the police that he wasn't going to press charges and they let me go after three days with a warning. They gave me a warning and told me to stay off the streets and get a job. I walked the streets looking for you but never found you. I was so tired and hungry; I went into a church and slept on a pew. A man who had been working there found me asleep and woke me up. He asked me what I was doing there. I told him I was cold and hungry and had nowhere to go. He laughed at me "Just like Mary and Joseph" I had no idea what he meant. He asked me where I lived and I told him that Dad had locked me out and that I was looking for you, and that you had nowhere to go either. I was bawling like a baby. He took me home for a meal. His wife reminded me of Mom. I can't believe she is dead. I so wanted to see her again" Then he asked where his father was. Bobby told him that he had taken off the day their mother died and they hadn't heard from him since. "He was a beast," Thomas hissed. Grandma sobbed audibly and when Thomas realized what he had said and went over to her "I am so sorry Grandma, can I really call you that?" Grandma patted his arm and told him she knew all about her son and he was a beast. I just pray that the good Lord will forgive him. You are a dear boy, and I am so glad to meet you" They exchanged facts about themselves for a long time then Thomas said that he and

Paula would have to go. Bobby took them back to the college and told them to call anytime they wanted to come over and he would pick them up. Alone in their room they talked to each other about the amazing workings of God, in their lives and wondered what else He had in store for them

Bobby, home again looked at Joe and shook his head. "Unbelievable" was all he could say. He had not been this emotional since he had lost his sisters. I wish you could all stay here, but Tommy is going back to work for Paula's dad and you don't know where you will be going. "I am pretty sure that I am going to get a medical discharge according to the doctors, I just need to find a job and then somewhere to live. I would love to stay in this area." "You could work for me, that is, if you would want to". I own the hardware store down near where we used to live, you know on the way to our school." I would love that. I am a good worker, people call me slow but that's because I like to do things right, so I think a lot before I do anything." Bobby put his arm around Joe being careful not to hurt him again. "Nothing would make me happier" "Now lets get your back attended to and we can read the Scriptures together before we go to bed." Later when Anna and he were getting ready for bed, she said that Ruthie's counselor had called and more or less insisted that Ruthie continue with counseling. Anna had told her that Ruthie was doing so well that she didn't think it was necessary for her to continue. The social worker more or less told her that she didn't know what she was talking about, and so Anna had told her that they would arrange for private counseling. Bobby said, "Do you know someone who would be helpful to Ruthie?" Anna grinned and said "Well I had the Pastor in mind" Bobby agreed that she was right .He thought that it was an excellent idea and said that he would talk to the pastor the following day. "Sleep well; you have not been sleeping much these last few nights. Just be thankful for everything. God is in control." "I wonder where Lillie and our father are, and. I wonder how I will react if I ever meet him" "God will give you the grace when the time comes, so don't be worrying about it now." He agreed and thanked her for her support and said goodnight.

As he drifted off to sleep he thought about how much easier it was to accept things as they happen when he trusted God. He was looking forward to spending time with his brothers. He was so happy that they were both Christians. He thought about a song he and Anna sang sometimes. It was one written in 1855, by Joseph Scriven.

What a friend we have in Jesus
All our sins and griefs to bear.
What a privilege to carry
Everything to God in prayer.
Are we weak and heavy laden?
Cumbered with a load of care
All because we do not carry
Everything to God in prayer.

He had proved this repeatedly. He said a silent prayer of thanks to God for all that He had done in his life. He thought about his mother's prayers for each of her children and wished that he could tell her that everything was turning out all right. He felt that his life was a testimony of God's wonderful mercy and grace. He thanked God again for his wife who supported him in every way, and for His grandmother and Ruthie, his sweet little daughter Ruthann, and his brothers.

The following days were unsettling for Bobby. He thought more and more about his father. He had successfully put him out of his mind for many years. Now he found himself wrestling with the thoughts of forgiveness. He found it hard to concentrate on work. He wondered what he would do if His father showed up next. He did not know how he would react if he met him again. He knew all about forgiveness. God had forgiven him, after all, but could he forgive the man who had killed his mother? He read the Scriptures at lunchtime and read about David. The Bible said that David was a man after God's own heart. He was loved of God and he had killed and done other awful things. He supposed forgiveness would depend on whether or not his father had repented; or did it. Repentance was his father's problem but forgiveness was his own. He thought again, about how God had sent His Son to die for the sins of many. Was his father one of those? He arranged with his staff so that he could leave the store for a while and he called the pastor, to see if he had time to talk. The pastor told him to come on over. When he got there he found Peter there, and he was very concerned about something. The pastor told Bobby that Peter had been recalled already and would be leaving in two weeks time. He was worried about Joe. "He seems ok, but all his doctors told us that he needed company for a while to be sure that he was ok." "No problem, He can stay with us. We have plenty of room. We would love to have him." "The docs said that he may get depressed and to keep an eye on him. I think God will take care of him but I did promise the docs." "Don't worry about a thing. He is going to come and work with me at the store, so I will be there with him. Can I cancel the rental agreement, then?" "By all means, yes, he can stay where he is; he will be just fine. "Thanks a million, I owe my life to that guy, and I hate to leave him." Peter shook hands with Bobby and left. Bobby asked his pastor if he would meet with Ruthie and told him about the social worker's insistence on counseling. The pastor said he would be glad to and would count it a privilege to do this for his sister. Then he told the pastor about his feelings about forgiveness.

The pastor told him that most people had a problem with things like that. He told Bobby a story of a man, whose young daughter had been murdered by a neighbor. After the trial, which was extremely difficult for him, he was walking to his car one day when the wife of the neighbor in question, walked up to him. She told him how sorry she was for what her husband had done. She was weeping and he was moved by her sorrow. She told him that she was going to move away because none of their neighbors would speak to her, and would not serve her at the grocery store. She was very unhappy but could not think of anything she could do to fix the awful thing her husband had done. He took her hand and prayed with her, right there in the street. Then he escorted her to the grocery store and told her to fetch her groceries. He paid for them himself. He saw the far-reaching effects of unforgiveness, and God touched his heart. He saw the woman home and told her not to leave on his account. He went to each of his neighbors and told them that he had forgiven the man who had killed his child. At the sentencing, he asked to make a statement. He told the man who had taken his child from him that he forgave him. The murderer was so moved that he broke down and cried in the court. He was sentenced to twenty years without parole. That man went to visit him in prison every month and eventually God opened the wicked heart of that man and saved him. The little girl's father rejoiced with him and when asked why he did what he did, he said, "We have a merciful God who gave his son so that others might live. I could do no less. I have peace in my heart where bitterness might have grown. I have love in my heart where hatred might have lived. I miss my little girl but hatred would not have brought her back, and many others would have suffered. God has given me the grace to do this. I do it in His strength not my own." The pastor told Bobby that God would enable him, and that he did not have to wait until his father showed up to forgive him. He needed to do it now. They prayed together and asked God to give Bobby whatever he needed to do God's will.

On the way home Bobby realized that with all the gifts, which God had given him, came responsibilities to do whatever God asked. He knew in his heart that God wanted him to forgive his father; so silently by the side of the road He bowed his head and surrendered his hatred of his father to Christ. He felt as if a great burden had been lifted from him. He had thought all these years that he had put all the things that had happened before his mother died, behind him but now he realized that they had all been stuffed into a dark corner of his heart where they could pop out at any time. He was glad that they were finally put to rest and he had joy in his heart once more.

Although the next few years did not bring Lillie back as he had hoped, he was thankful for everything, which God had done for him. He saw Ruthie blossom into a beautiful young woman who did very well in school and started looking towards college. Joseph was an excellent employee and eventually Bobby gave him part ownership of the store. Tommy did well and he and his wife came back often to visit. Anna gave Bobby the joyful news that he was to be a father again. God blessed his ministry with the youth and he saw many of them come to know the Lord Jesus as their Savior. All in all life was good for Robert Swanson, brother, husband, father, youth leader, and godly young man.

CPSIA information can be obtained at www.ICGtesting.com
230205LV00004B/19/P